On Edge

By Russ Crossley

53rd Street Publishing

Offices in Gibsons, B.C. Canada, and Lincoln City, Oregon

Dedication

I dedicate this book to the late Gene Roddenberry for his vision of a hopeful future for humankind. Thanks, Gene.

Acknowledgments

Many thanks to my first reader, Rita Schulz, and my editor, Colleen Kuhne, for their invaluable insights into these stories. They make me a far better writer than I truly am. Thank you, ladies.

On Edge

Russ Crossley

Published by 53rd Street Publishing
Copyright 2015 Russ Crossley
All rights reserved

Cover art © Dmytro Tolokonov |
Cover designed by R. Edgewood
Cover design and layout copyright 2015 by 53rd
Street Publishing

ISBN 9781927621448

53rd Street Publishing
Head office: Gibsons B.C. Canada
www.53rdstreetpublishing.com

Table of Contents

Introduction

I have been a fan of science fiction in all its forms since I was a child. I watched every cheesy giant bug/monster movie I could see on my black and white TV screen. I read all sorts of comic books, magazines, and eventually science fiction novels I could get at my local library. I listened to recordings of old radio programs that were broadcast before I was born if they had any fantastic element (X-1 is still my favorite).

I recall the first time I saw an episode of Star Trek and nearly fell off my chair my eyes wide as saucers, my heart beating rapidly. This was the science fiction I had dreamed of as I watched the reality of man's first steps into space during the Mercury, Gemini and Apollo rocket launches to the eventual first steps on the surface of our moon. This sense of wonder and excitement has never left me to this day.

Science fiction today is shinier and more spectacular with all the dazzling movie wizardry available today and private companies have now begun to launch spacecraft into orbit. Times and technology may have changed but wonder and excitement of the unknown still drives the human race to continue to create stories of the fantastic.

This collection is my love letter to a genre I love created with wonder and imagination of a true fan. So open the book and enjoy these five tales as much I as I did in creating them.

Russ Crossley
Gibsons, B.C.

Neighborhood Watch

THE FLICKERING FLAME from the oil lamp cast twisted, writhing shadows over the walls of Pete Simpson's recreation room in the basement of his split-level, four-bedroom house. The large room was a real man cave. Even after all this time, the room still smelled of cigar smoke and beer, though we hadn't had either of those luxuries since this all began six weeks ago. We four neighborhood watch members were seated around a seven-player mahogany poker table. The playing surface was covered in a tobacco-colored leather, with integrated chip wells and cup holders. We were waiting for the arrival of the fifth member of our group. Seven armless, matching leather chairs surrounded the table.

Only we weren't here to play poker.

Neighborhood Watch

Along the walls of the oblong-shaped room were burnished steel shelves containing trophies and plaques from Pete's days as a high school and state collegiate athlete. Amongst these personal treasures were his sports collectibles signed baseballs, basketballs, and footballs representing every pro team in the state of Washington and in Portland, Oregon, just across the Columbia River.

In a wide gap in the bookshelves was a sixty-inch flat screen television. Facing the large digital TV were two rows of leather recliners, five chairs in each row. The simulated oak flooring stood up to the punishment of Sunday NFL games and final four weekends.

Pete hadn't been a star amongst his athletic peers but he had been pretty good. Too bad for him, others were better. They received the scholarships while Pete became a used car salesman who lived in our middle class neighborhood on the outskirts of Vancouver. He was trapped in suburbia along with the rest of us.

Of course, his collectibles and trophies were worthless now. No one is going to barter for a can of tuna with a collectible anymore, not when cash money, gold, and diamonds have no value. Especially when you and your family will starve to death without food. Food and water meant survival.

How ironic it was that we'd wasted our lives striving for now worthless *stuff*.

"Where's Oscar?" asked Alice, who was seated across from me, her dark eyes narrowed to slits. She was constantly wringing her hands as if washing them. Her short brown hair was oily and she reeked of sour sweat, but then, didn't we all? None of us had had enough water to shower or bathe for weeks now. We'd thought about going to the river, but being outside our barricaded neighborhood was risky and presented serious security issues for us.

My poor friend, Alice, was nervous and becoming increasingly edgy over the past few days. Recent events had brought us all to the edge of our sanity.

The lacquered pine paneling that lined the walls behind the shelves had always bothered me. Who in their right mind would keep this cheap '60s crap on their walls? I rolled my eyes since I knew the answer without asking the question. A Neanderthal like Pete, seated to my right, of course. With his thinning hair and receding hairline and expanding beer gut, he had become the poster boy around the neighborhood for the fading athlete. Now, of course, he was a shriveled man—half his former size, with sunken, grizzled cheeks.

Neighborhood Watch

"Got the time?" I asked Conrad, seated across the table from me. He looked at his mechanical watch and his lips formed a grim, humorless line. "He's more than an hour overdue."

I slapped Pete's left shoulder with the back of my hand. "I thought you said he'd be back with the scouting party by now?"

Pete scowled at me, his piercing cobalt eyes angry. "Knock it off, Liz, I'm as worried about them as you are. We *all* know the risks."

"Yeah," I said, sweeping stray lengths of my scraggly, dirty-blonde hair away from over my eyes with my arm. I hadn't had a decent haircut in weeks and had decided earlier today to shave my head completely as many of the neighborhood women and some men had done, although I loved my long hair. It had taken years to grow it this long.

"But they promised us we had ninety days," said May. "Surely we can last at least that long." May was Chinese-American, with dark, almond-shaped eyes that seemed to look right through you, and high cheekbones. She'd always been thin but now her bare arms looked skeletal in her sleeveless, pink, cotton top.

I gritted my teeth as my guts twisted.

4

May's words tore through me like a knife, but I knew she was right. The voluntary ration system wasn't working. Individual greed had overcome the greater good. We were failing. The truth, I knew, was not greed but survival, a very human instinct in these circumstances. People in the neighborhood had been hoarding supplies for themselves, not sharing as we had all agreed.

At the neighborhood watch meeting convened a week after they arrived and cut off the power, representatives from every house in our subdivision agreed to work for the common good. Now that supplies were becoming scarce, it was becoming obvious not everyone was sharing everything.

If Oscar and his small force of four men and two women didn't return from the latest mission, it was bad news for the neighborhood. Several times, food- and medicine-scrounging missions had disappeared in the past two weeks. These volunteers were sent out heavily armed, with guns collected from the neighborhood residents for a collective armory. Their unexplained disappearance meant conditions outside the barricades we'd set up after the power grid failed were getting worse, or something too terrible to contemplate was happening.

Neighborhood Watch

Our role as neighborhood leaders may have also broken down. I wished now Oscar hadn't agreed to lead this last mission himself, but he had explained that we as leaders needed to lead and show the people we accepted the same risks as everyone else.

Before he left, he told me privately he'd determine what had happened to the other teams if he could.

If our leadership failed to maintain control, then we'd fall into anarchy, survival of the fittest would surpass all other considerations, and we'd have a crisis on our hands. The thought of quelling an uprising of my friends and neighbors caused me many sleepless nights.

A few of the neighborhood men were former military, or reservists like Pete, who had skills with weapons. Many of these qualified former soldiers were manning the makeshift barricades, composed of trucks and cars that had been abandoned after the fuel supply was gone and various pieces of furniture, surrounding the perimeter of the ten block radius we were responsible for. So far, our internal communications system had been working.

We'd been using old analog, battery-operated walkie-talkies, but the supply of batteries, as with the food and water, was nearly exhausted.

Our neighborhood consisted of fifty homes originally containing two hundred and twenty-five residents. In the past six weeks, we'd lost thirty-five in total. Fifteen disappeared on supply missions, an equal number of the elderly and the very young were lost to starvation, suicides made up the balance of our losses. We were down to one hundred ninety warm bodies. Many were physically capable but I wasn't so sure about many of these peoples mental state.

Suddenly we heard footsteps pounding down the stairs from above us and Sue Burns burst into to the room, her breath coming in gasps, her lean arms and bare legs covered in a sheen of sweat. Her tan shorts and white top were sweat stained and greasy. Her green eyes were wild and unfocused by fear.

In her trembling right hand she held a walkie-talkie. In her left was the AR-15 semi-auto rifle I had given her after she completed firearms training two weeks ago.

"Sue," I said in a voice meant to calm her. "Calm down."

Sue nodded but her eyes flitted between the assembled leaders still seated at the table and she was avoiding making eye contact with me. Her breathing steadied but her worn Nikes still shifted side to side.

Neighborhood Watch

The woman was as jumpy as a cat on summer-heated blacktop.

I stood, then placed my hands on the sides of her narrow shoulders to steady her and stared into her eyes. "What's wrong, Sue?"

She finally looked at me, but her eyes were placid and eerily free of any emotion I could recognize. It was as if she was now at the center of a hurricane. "Uhhhh...there's a group of armed people approaching the north side of the barricades near Elmont Street," she said, her voice a dry hoarse whisper.

My breath caught in my throat. I looked over my shoulder at Pete, who had visibly tensed. "You and the others go ahead and check it out. I'll be along shortly."

Pete's tanned brow wrinkled and his eyes narrowed. He stood and signaled to the others to stand, too, then nodded. He hurried up the stairs with May and Alice close behind. I heard the echo of their footsteps *thump* up the stairs until there again was silence. Before they left the house, they would arm themselves and then head for the Elmont Street barricade.

I directed my attention to studying Sue's sweaty features. Her shoulders sagged and I knew the adrenaline driving her was ebbing.

Russ Crossley

I gently took the walkie-talkie from her and set it on the poker table. I then slipped my fingers around the barrel of the rifle gripped in her left hand, intending to take it from her as well.

Sue's normally placid, oval-shaped face shifted to anger, her eyes glaring at me. I sensed the strength returning to her lean frame. She pulled the gun away violently, forcing me to reluctantly release the weapon. In her present state, Sue was probably dangerous to herself and others.

This was confirmed when I saw the look in her eyes and knew she had lost touch with reality. For the first time since the beginning of the crisis, it occurred to me that a neighbor might shoot me. "Sue, tell me what's wrong." I spoke in an even tone so as not to spook her.

"I need the gun," she said between gritted teeth. I stepped back and gave her room, raising my hands in surrender.

"Why don't you sit and we'll talk?"

Sue's eyes narrowed and a bead of sweat ran down her sunburned cheek. "You're trying to trick me. You want my gun." She pointed the muzzle at me, her right index finger hovering over the trigger. "I will kill you...anyone...who tries to take my gun." Her voice was low and threatening.

Neighborhood Watch

I smiled and sat down, placing my hands, one over the other, on the table and resting my weight on my forearms. "No, of course I won't take your gun. If you recall, I was the one who gave it to you." I kept my tone light.

Sue's features twisted in confusion, anger, and suspicion all at once. I'd succeeded in confusing her. Slowly she lowered the gun and dropped into the chair across from me, the AR-15 hanging loose at her side, the barrel pointed at the floor. She appeared exhausted, the last of her inner resources spent. A sense of relief washed over me.

I walked around the table until I stood beside her slumping body. Her eyelids were heavy with sleep. I carefully reached for the rifle and managed to gingerly release her now loose grip when she suddenly bolted upright, grabbing for the barrel. I pulled hard and wrested it away from her as she managed to stand, her face twisted by inner fury. Waves of intense hatred from Sue washed over me. I knew, if she managed to keep control of the gun, I was dead and then the others would be next. I had to take it from her. I had no choice.

It was as if the world was moving in slow motion. I took two steps backward as I raised the gun until it was level with her midsection.

Without thinking, I pulled the trigger twice. Two loud bangs echoed off the walls and Sue's eyes went wide as she stumbled backward, gasping for breath. My nostrils and mouth were suddenly invaded by the smell of burnt gunpowder mingled with the iron scent of blood.

Sue clutched her stomach with both hands. Dark red blood seeped between her fingers. I froze. She looked at me, her eyes wide, the pain behind them making me want to wretch. I couldn't believe I'd shot my friend. *God, what have I done?*

I lowered the weapon, letting it fall from my grip. It rattled as it struck the floor. "Sue, I'm so sorry."

Sue's mouth hung open as blood started to trickle from the right side of her mouth. She dropped to her knees, then collapsed onto her bottom with a cry of pain. She moaned softly. I knelt beside her and wrapped one arm around her shoulders as she dropped backward. I sat on the floor, cradling her head in my lap. She looked up at me, her watery eyes filled with pain. Her mouth moved but I couldn't make out most of the words except for "Sorry."

Her eyes closed and her head lolled to one side as the air escaped from her lungs for the last time. I hugged her to me and began to cry, salty tears rolling down my cheeks.

Neighborhood Watch

"I'm sorry, so sorry, Susie, I didn't...." I was about to say I didn't mean to kill her, but that wasn't true. I'd had to stop her even if it meant killing her. It was like shooting a rabid dog. Sue had gone off the mental cliff and she wouldn't have come back. She could have killed us all.

I eased her off my lap and let her limp body roll on its side in the pool of blood that had formed around her before her heart stopped. I wiped the tears away from my eyes and stood.

A rush of anger formed a knot in my belly. Those bastards were at fault. *They* forced us to turn on each other. A lot of good people, a lot of Sue's, would still be alive if they hadn't come to our planet. *Goddamned aliens*.

***

The cement floor of the warehouse made the interior of the vast empty building cooler than the humid air outside. I had my eyes closed as I fanned myself with one hand, grateful for the relief from the oppressive summer heat bearing down on the harbor beyond the open bay doors lining both sides of the structure. The warehouse sat at the end of a long pier, jutting out into the bay.

Russ Crossley

A cry of gulls filled my ears. I opened my eyes
to gaze out the open bay door nearest me and spotted
the gray wings of the snow-white birds circling
above the overturned and burned-out ships floating
untended in the oily water in the bay. Like the water,
the air was still; but I could smell the rotting flesh
of dead fish and human corpses entombed in those
shattered vessels. The stench used to make me gag but
I was well past that now—I was getting used to the
odors of death. I'd seen too much of it in the past six
weeks, more than most soldiers saw in a year on the
battlefield. But we were on the frontline of the fight
for survival, and one consequence was witnessing
things no one should have to.

"Liz," called a man's voice from behind my left
shoulder. I shifted on the steel chair to face him—Al
Hamburg, in his battle armor, hefting his assault
rifle. His curly blond hair stuck out from the edges
of a Kevlar helmet and dark sunglasses covered his
eyes. His torso, arms, and legs were protected by
body armor. He nodded at me when I didn't reply and
disappeared from view behind the warehouse wall
where he would stand guard until he escorted me back
to the neighborhood. We were five miles from the
barricades but I knew Al and his team would protect
me.

They had accompanied me from the barricade, where they'd shown up to escort me to this meeting. Professional soldiers always follow orders, so I wasn't worried.

Al was the commander of an elite Special Forces unit recruited by the Hsu-Zat to act as bodyguards when they visited our planet's surface. The Hsu-Zat had arrived in Earth orbit six weeks ago and immediately used some form of advanced electromagnetic pulse weapon to take out our technology worldwide. The weapon even used our satellites to send the pulse that threw civilization back into the dark ages. I missed my damned cell phone more than I should. I must have been addicted to the thing.

Airliners dropped from the sky, creating massive destruction and loss of life. Military forces so dependent on technology found themselves and their weapons useless. Even the most EMP-hardened technology was ineffective in preventing this alien weapon from taking it out. The world had gone all to hell, and all that stood between anarchy and order was the neighborhood watch.

I know all this because, for some reason, a Hsu-Zat who called himself Robert—he told me his real name would be unpronounceable—decided I would be the spokesperson for my neighborhood. We'd met regularly, once per week, for the past six weeks. I'd never asked why he chose me, and frankly I didn't care.

The odd thing was Robert answered any question I asked him and had since our first meeting. As far as I could tell, everything he told me was accurate. The human tendency to lie to protect personal feelings didn't seem to apply to these aliens. He casually related the death toll numbers caused by their suppression of our technology and by the disruptions in civil order that soon followed.

If he considered my circumstances dire in any way, he hadn't let on. In fact, Robert had been cold but not unkind to me. That's why I'd left my knife behind, the one I had intended to use to slit his throat as retribution for Sue's death. Even if I managed to kill him, one alien's death wouldn't mean much in the scheme of things.

From one of the open bay doors, Robert entered, flanked by two others of his kind.

Neighborhood Watch

His crimson-colored features were placid, his two mustard-yellow eyes avoiding me as his brown boots slapped the concrete floor. The sound of the three aliens' footsteps echoed off the high walls. Other than their skin color, they were humanoid: two arms, two legs, everything in the same places as us. It had been difficult for me to distinguish one alien from another until I noticed the small scar on the end of Robert's pointed chin. He later told me this was due to a childhood fall without elaborating further.

His dark blue slacks and brown vest covered a frame that looked lean and strong, yet his voice had always been gentle, reminding me of the sound of a stream rushing over a rocky bottom. His arms were bare, as was his hairless head. His ears were relatively human shaped, the curvature at the top slightly elongated. His companions were dressed in identical garb. *There must have been a big sale on alien fashions at the Hsu-Zat Walmart.*

Robert stopped in front of me. His long arms, hanging loosely at his sides, ended with elongated fingers near his knees. Neither he nor his escorts had even been seen carrying weapons. *Ray guns obviously aren't his team's thing.*

One of his escorts went to grab another steel chair from ten feet across the warehouse floor.

He carried it back, placing it behind Robert, who immediately sat, his eyes finally landing on mine.

"Hello, Elizabeth," he said in his usual monotone.

"Robert," I said with a slight nod of my head.

His eyes crinkled slightly at the corners. "I am saddened to learn of Susan's death."

I don't know how he knew, but Al probably told him before the meeting. I had learned not to trust those Special Forces guys. As far as I was concerned, they were the aliens' pets.

His words seemed genuine. Robert had either won the Hsu-Zat equivalent of the best actor Oscar or he meant what he'd said. I prefer to think it was the latter because he had never before shown any remorse for the deaths they had caused. At our next meeting, I decided, I would reverse my earlier decision. This son of a bitch was dead. I would probably die too, but the satisfaction would be better than a gold card with an unlimited credit limit.

"I am leaving," Robert said next.

"But you just got here," I said sarcastically.

Robert hesitated and his eyes shifted to an open bay door to his right and the ocean beyond. I glanced out the door. The wind had picked up and small swells had formed in the harbor. The cooling breeze brushed my right cheek.

Neighborhood Watch

I detected the now familiar smells of almonds and orange coming from the aliens as the wind swirled through the warm air of the warehouse.

Robert's yellow eyes finally drifted back to mine. "Please forgive me. I meant we are leaving for home earlier than expected."

May's words echoed in my mind and my heart skipped a beat. "You said we had ninety days then you'd turn the power back on."

Robert nodded. "Yes, I did, but my orders have changed. I must return home immediately." The alien stared at me, his eyes pleading. He was unable to elaborate. I glanced at his companions and saw them standing stiff as soldiers at attention, their eyes focused straight ahead looking into the distance, appearing uninterested in our conversation. But I knew they were very interested and listening to every word.

"Will you at least turn the power back on?"

Robert shook his head. "No, that is beyond our capability."

I pursed my lips as my gut tightened. The bastards told us when they destroyed the grids they would restore them after ninety days. It hadn't made sense at the time, but what choice did we have but to believe them. Obviously they lied. "When are you leaving?"

"Immediately," he said again. He paused and I could tell his next words were very uncomfortable for him. I braced myself for the worst. "There are nuclear power generating facilities all across your world that are going critical without the power grid. These facilities will soon melt down and send clouds of radioactive material into your atmosphere. Unfortunately, this means all life on your planet will be extinguished."

My stomach churned and my emotions threatened to overwhelm me. Fear, anger, love, hate ebbed and flowed through my mind. "Then what was the ninety days all about?"

For the first time since I'd met him, Robert appeared flustered. His features were a darker red, his skin now the color of pomegranate juice. His hands trembled and his eyes sagged, reflecting a very human sadness. "I'm sorry," he said again. "Orders."

I nodded and sighed. He wasn't a bad guy for an alien. "Okay, Robert." I stood and his two companions suddenly stepped between us. I smirked at the three aliens, then turned and walked away.

The ninety days was in realty a countdown. A countdown to doomsday. The Hsu-Zat had known all along what would happen after they shut down everything.

Neighborhood Watch

Their arrival was an experiment and we were the guinea pigs.

Once the human race was extinct, the aliens would eventually have a green and fertile planet to colonize without interference from the indigenous population. Sure, it would take time for the Earth's ecosystems to regenerate, but the Hsu Zat had all time in the universe. Our time had run out. Maybe Sue was one of the lucky ones.

I was determined to delay our impending doom, at least in my little corner of the world. The neighborhood watch would continue maintaining some semblance of civilization until the end came. We weren't going quietly into the night.

While it was more likely we'd destroy ourselves before the radioactive clouds killed us, the neighborhood watch would forestall the inevitable as long as possible. Our neighborhood would stand alone if need be.

As for me, I was determined to be the leader I was born to be. I wasn't about to give the Hsu Zat our neighborhood without showing them we still had fight left in us. It's what we humans do.

A Father's Daughter

Saffron shifted her bottom on the hard pine chair, where she sat studying the unadorned steel-gray walls and floor of the ten-by-ten-foot room surrounding the burnished steel desk in the center of the otherwise bare room. Looking down at herself, she discovered she was dressed in black slacks, flats, and a white cotton long-sleeved shirt. The clothes reminded her of the K-Mart housewives she silently mocked when she made trips to the mall to visit the high-end shops for new shoes and the latest fashions. She had closets reserved just for her shoes. She had never worn such frumpy clothes in her life.

Seated across from her in a brown, well-worn leather chair, was a pale-faced, severe-looking woman with mint green eyes, her angular features focused on the pages of a large, clothbound book, open on the desk in front of her.

A Father's Daughter

Saffron had no sense of how long she'd been here or how she'd gotten here. But she did have a vague sense of unease, deep in her belly, that had formed a knot reminiscent of hunger.

Yet she wasn't hungry, at least not exactly, as she thought of hunger. In the recesses of her mind, memoires bubbled of the taste of champagne and cherries and coffee, but she had no compulsion or need for them. Something had changed. But what?

Saffron's auburn eyes finally landed on the woman across from her, who smelled of peppermints and chamomile tea like her grandmother, who had died when she and her twin sister, Sadie, were fifteen years old. Their father had taken them with him to retrieve her grandmother's clothes for the funeral. She recalled seeing the hairbrush lying face up on her grandmother's antique mirrored dresser, the battleship-gray wisps of hair still clinging to the stiff, black horsehair bristles as if trapped for eternity as the only remaining evidence of the woman who gave her chocolate candies at Christmas, and sent crisp, new dollar bills for her and her sister in a birthday card each year.

A twinge of regret for the unkindness toward her elderly grandmother invaded her thoughts briefly, then retreated immediately.

As long as she could recall, her grandmother had been trapped in a frail body twisted by painful arthritis. Saffron had been young and stupid then, a horribly self-absorbed teenager who failed to appreciate her elders.

Her deepest regret was reserved for her father, whose angry eyes bore into her when, at her grandmother's funeral, she and her sister had giggled at some inane private joke between them.

Mercifully he never spoke to her about the incident, but she knew they had disappointed him. Her beloved father was the only man she had ever looked to for wisdom and guidance. Most of the men she dated were spoiled pretty-boys with more money than brains. They definitely weren't the type of men she would ever marry or turn to for advice.

She had always wanted to apologize to her father for her behavior, but had never had the courage to bring up the subject with him. Since that day, she'd considered their relationship irrecoverably damaged.

Looking around the bare room, she somehow sensed that her opportunity to tell her father how she felt had passed.

"Miss Smythe?" said the woman, startling her from her moment of retrospection.

The woman's voice had a deep timber and an edge of disapproval. Hanging from her neck by a thin chain was a pair of horn-rimmed glasses. She was wearing a dowdy dress of navy-blue roses over a pale beige background. A button at the neck secured the collar. Her dark hair was shot through with gray streaks and was tied into a bun atop her narrow head.

"Yes. Saffron Smythe, actually."

One pepper-colored eyebrow arched on her pale forehead as she regarded Saffron, obviously unimpressed. "Yes," she said, "Saffron, of course." The woman interlaced her long, tapered fingers on top of the pages of the open book, then leaned slightly forward, her elbows resting on the book. Her dispassionate gaze made Saffron uncomfortable. "According to our records, you are here slightly earlier than expected."

"Ummmm, that's the thing, Ms...." Saffron looked at the woman questioningly.

"Ruth. You may call me Ruth." A slight hitch in Ruth's tone suggested Saffron was to continue. She had a small, humorless smile on her lips.

Saffron nodded. "I'm not sure where I am, exactly."

The woman nodded, unlaced her fingers, and eased back in her chair, her expression sending

Saffron signals that she had heard this question many times. "Of course. Many who arrive here have no idea their existence on Earth is at an end."

Saffron froze and her jaw dropped. She shivered as if she was suddenly chilled, except the room's temperature was nearly perfect. "Do you mean I'm dead?"

A sardonic smile spread across Ruth's features. "Yes. But don't be concerned. You're in the best of hands. I'll soon have your next assignment ready."

"But I can't be dead," Saffron whispered. "I'm too young. And I'm too rich."

Ruth grinned. "I hear that *a lot,* more often than you might think, actually."

Anger bubbled up from Saffron's stomach. She tasted sour bile at the back of her throat. *How can I be dead and still taste bile*? She sucked in a breath, then exhaled. *I seem to be breathing.* She pinched the skin of her right arm between thumb and forefinger as hard as she could, and winced at the sudden rush of pain. *Son of a bi—* She spat her next words between gritted teeth. "Lady, I don't know who you are, but I'm the daughter of a very powerful man, so I suggest you let me go immediately."

"Oh, but Saffron, no one is holding you here, I assure you. This is a way station."

"My job is to prepare you for your final destination."

Saffron's anger subsided and she eyed the woman. "Final destination?" She had a bad feeling about Ruth's answer. She knew somehow she wouldn't like it.

A sardonic grin came over Ruth's pale features and her eyes narrowed. "Yes," Ruth said simply, offering no further explanation.

Saffron tried to recall where she had been and what she had been doing before realizing she was in this windowless room across a desk from this woman who reeked of peppermints. No matter how she tried, it was as if her mind was in a fog.

"It's okay, Saffron. It's unlikely you'll be able to recall anything from the time before you died except for flashes of stray thoughts that may seem like dreams. But don't be concerned. This is often taxing on new arrivals at first, but with time, you will understand. Most new arrivals find that when they are allowed into the hall of memories, they begin to comprehend what they had been in life and what they are now." Ruth spoke as if these cryptic words made perfect sense; however, Saffron remained thoroughly confused.

This lady is nutso. "Okay, I get it, I'm dead and this is heaven...but how did I die?" Saffron suddenly froze when an image formed of herself lying in a bathtub, buried in an ocean of white foam. She was somehow hovering over herself, looking down at her naked form through the dissipating bubbles, lying on her back under the water in the marble tub. Her body was limp, unmoving, her eyes closed. Saffron realized the *her* in the bathtub wasn't breathing and the lips were pale, the skin on the face a sickly gray pallor. A half empty crystal champagne flute sat on the edge of the tub. The bubbles in the wine having long ago dispersed meant the flute had sat untouched for too long and gone flat.

It dawned on her she had died while having a bubble bath.

She loved bubble baths, the water lapping against her skin like a silk blanket, the warm steam rising from the white jasmine-scented bubbles. Surely she wasn't meant to die in a bath? Saffron licked her lips. *I loved the taste of champagne on my tongue.*

Ruth laughed lightly, causing the corners of her eyes to crinkle. "No, this isn't heaven. As I said before, this is a way station where you will receive your next assignment."

Saffron studied the woman's placid features, then her eyes dropped to look at the book. "What's in the book?" she asked.

"This is a record of each person's date of death. My job is to fill in the column listing each arrival's final destination—once I'm told, of course."

Saffron's eyes narrowed. "Told? Told by whom?"

Suddenly a telephone began to emit a muffled ring. Ruth smiled and reached down to open a drawer in the desk beside her. She withdrew a telephone as black as licorice, with a heavy black wire trailing off the back of the unit and a dial face on the front, covering a white background depicting large numbers and small block letters under each opening in the dial. There was a receiver in a cradle on the top, attached the main body by a wire. As Ruth set it on the desk with a soft *thump*, it rang again, only louder this time since the drawer didn't muffle it.

Saffron had never seen a telephone like it. Where was Ruth's cell phone?

Ruth picked up the receiver and held it to her ear. "Yes?" She listened intently to whomever had called, her expression changing from pleased, to concern, to puzzlement. Finally she said good-bye and hung up. Her eyes reflected her astonishment.

She sighed before she spoke. "This happens so rarely I am surprised every time it does." Ruth paused, adding to Saffron's discomfort. Finally she continued. "I'm advised you are to be sent back to Earth."

She paused again to look into Saffron's eyes since they must have revealed her excitement.

I'm going home.

"I'm sorry, I'm not being clear. Your spirit will be sent to Earth, but your interaction with living beings will be quite limited." Ruth cleared her throat, Saffron sensing the woman's hesitation. "It appears you have indeed arrived earlier than expected because you were murdered."

Oh, shit. I'm in trouble. I need Amanda Dark.

* * *

Saffron had no sense of movement but she suddenly materialized in Phillip Swann's office, one of many in the law offices of Smythe, Wellington, Goldberg, and Thompson. Her senses were immediately assaulted by the scent of wood polish, which wasn't surprising as the Boston law firm had never removed the original teak paneling since the prestigious firm opened in 1902.

Such expensive wood required constant care to maintain its gleaming, pristine appearance, but the partners agreed it added to the firm's elegant image. The firm had represented Boston's social elite worldwide for over a hundred years. Of course, she knew this because her great-great-great-grandfather had been the founder and an original partner of the firm. Her father still represented the family name on the masthead.

Before the way station disappeared as if in a fog, Ruth explained Saffron had been granted one visit outside the place she was to haunt until the matter of her murder was settled. By settled, of course, Ruth meant the murder was solved and the killer brought to justice. Only then would Saffron return to the way station to be assigned her final destination.

She would be able to interact with one living person and be able to experience sensory details of the environment around her since this might help trigger memories essential to solving the crime. Ruth ended by warning her it might take some time, so she must be patient.

As if looking through a veil of mist, Saffron saw Phillip Swann come into focus.

He was seated in a black leather executive chair behind a massive, fifty-year-old teak desk, examining documents one by one from a thick file. The wood of the desk was stained dark and polished to a gleaming shine under the light of the crystal chandelier in the ten-foot-high ceiling overhead. A silver executive telephone was to Phillip's right and a large, flat computer screen was to his left. Behind his desk and running the length of the long office wall were built-in bookcases containing volumes of law books. One wall was a floor-to-ceiling picture window overlooking the bustling city streets far below. The glass was tinted so it wasn't too bright in the offices, even on the sunniest of days.

But Saffron's attention was drawn to Amanda Dark, who was seated in a horseshoe-shaped leather chair, watching Phillip from the other side of his massive desk. Amanda was a short woman, just over five feet in height; of medium build, not buxom and not thin; with mouse-brown hair cut to brush her shoulders. Her pleasant features, wide set curious hazel eyes, and smallish nose meant she couldn't be described as beautiful, but she wasn't ugly, either. Right now Amanda's eyes gazed at Phillip with a look in them Saffron knew well.

The woman loved the firm's associate more than she was willing to admit.

With his jet-black, curly hair cut military short, his square jaw, and dimples in both cheeks when he smiled, Saffron well understood Phillip's appeal. His narrow waist and lightly muscled arms under his tailored suits and shirts told her he took care of his appearance, but then, any lawyer whose goal was to become a partner needed every weapon in his arsenal to get there. Phillip Swann was bright, personable, and good looking, so he'd surely make partner someday.

Saffron had met Phillip and Amanda at one of her father's mixers held in the office a couple of times a year. Normally she avoided such stuffy affairs, preferring to hit the many clubs and bars around Boston with peers her own age; but for some reason, that day she attended the party where she met the young, handsome associate and his unlikely wannabe girlfriend.

Amanda claimed to be a paranormal detective. She hadn't explained what the job entailed, but Saffron soon learned that the plain-speaking woman had helped Phillip on a number of difficult estate cases resulting in very grateful and very wealthy clients who paid considerable sums to the firm.

Once, after a few too many drinks, her father told her Amanda Dark was a ghost whisperer and that she could speak to the spirits of the dead. Saffron thought this nonsense; she didn't believe in ghosts.

But when Ruth asked who she would like to see on Earth, Saffron immediately asked for Amanda Dark. Even if she were a fake, she had helped some big cases for the firm so she had to have some talent for dealing with the paranormal—or she was the most successful grifter in history. Seeing Amanda's K-Mart wardrobe of gray cotton slacks, white, no-name brand runners, and sleeveless, mint-green rayon top didn't scream flourishing con artist. Saffron doubted the latter was true.

Suddenly Saffron froze as Amanda visibly stiffened. She was looking right at her, her eyes growing wide—not with fear but with surprise. *She sees me now.*

"Uh, Phil, we have a visitor," Amanda said in a low voice.

"Ummm," said Phillip, his attention focused on a document he was reading from the file folder. "Tell them I'm busy."

"It's not *that* kind of visitor," explained Amanda, her voice louder now.

Phillip stopped reading as his brow wrinkled and he looked up at Amanda. "A ghost?" he asked as if it were an every day occurrence. In fact, Saffron could swear his expression was one of annoyance. "In my office?" He shook his head. "No way. We've never had a ghost in my office. You must be mistaken."

Amanda shook her head, her eyes still locked on Saffron, who stood still with a tight grin on her lips. "In fact, I think it's Robert Smythe's daughter."

Phillip grunted. "Really? Which one?" He scanned the room. "I don't see anyone."

Amanda grunted, then turned her head to scowl at him as if he were a small child. "Really, Phil, do we have to go through this *again*?"

Phillip's shoulders relaxed and he grinned, the dimples in his cheeks deepening. "I'm kidding, Amanda. Surely by now you know when I'm joking?"

The tension in Amanda's body eased and she chuckled. "Sorry, Phil, but you know how I am about my work."

"Amanda," interrupted Saffron, "have you two finished your mating dance yet? I have a big problem I need your help with."

Amanda shifted her attention to Saffron. "Sorry, Ms. Smythe, Phil and I are so used to ghosts and we too often verbally spar in front of them."

Her hazel eyes flitted to a grinning Phillip Swann, who eased back in his chair while maintaining his silence, then back to her. "What can I do for you?"

These two seemed to be laughing at her. *I've been murdered, for God's sake.*

A knot of anger formed in her stomach. Old habits from her impetuous, over-privileged youth were going to be tougher to break than she thought. She could not deny in life she had been a rich, spoiled brat, but now that she was dead, she had vowed to be better in the afterlife.

She managed to push the anger away before she spoke. "Please call me Saffron. Ms. Smythe was my late mother, God rest her soul." She paused as the humor faded from Amanda's eyes. Saffron then blurted, "I've been murdered. I desperately need your help to catch the killer."

***

Saffron stood on the cold marble floor of the expansive foyer of Smythe Hall, Amanda beside her. The sweeping circular staircase curled up and into the distance to the upper floors of the ten-bedroom, ten-bathroom mansion.

A Father's Daughter

The floor-to-ceiling crushed-red-velvet drapes over the tall windows bordering the cool foyer were drawn shut, requiring the large crystal chandelier hanging twenty-five feet above their heads to be illuminated, even though it was early afternoon on a summer day. The musty air spoke of age and neglect. Saffron realized something had happened in her family home—something bad.

Amanda coughed to clear her throat. "Phil said your father agreed to meet me...I mean us."

"You didn't tell him about me, did you?"

Amanda shook her head. "If I did, do you think he would agree to see me?"

Saffron sighed. Of course Amanda was correct. If she told him she had spoken to his dead daughter, he'd have dismissed her as a kook after his money. Her father was a practical man if nothing else.

"I have a question."

Amanda looked at her with a curious expression. Saffron continued. "How can I be dead so long but only now become..." Her words trailed off. She couldn't say the word ghost it sounded ridiculous.

How long ago did I die? For the first time, it occurred to her to wonder how long she'd been dead.

"When did I die?"

Amanda's brow wrinkled. "Space and time are very different in the after life. Time isn't linear—"

She was about to explain more when somewhere overhead a generator suddenly whirred to life in the silent, dusty air that stank of stale coffee and burnt toast interrupting them. Amanda eyes suggested that later might be a better time to talk.

Reluctantly Saffron agreed. She had a sense time was short, even though in reality she had more time now than she'd ever had in life.

Saffron saw a slit of light coming from the bottom of a closet door on the left side of the foyer that, as she recalled, contained her mother's and father's long evening coats.

The slit of light grew brighter as a rumbling sound and the whine of the generator increased in intensity. Finally there was a deep *thud* and the door of the closet slid aside to reveal a wizened man with white hair in a wheelchair. His gray eyes studied Amanda, his pale brow wrinkled by curiosity.

Saffron sucked in a breath as the man's long fingers worked a control stick on the right armrest of the wheelchair and it rolled out of the closet, now obviously converted to an elevator, onto the marble floor. Tears blurred her vision as she realized the man was her father.

A Father's Daughter

The once vital, healthy man who drank protein shakes for breakfast, ran in marathons, and worked out at the firm's gym three times a week had been replaced by these fossil-like remains.

Amanda's features were lit by a smile as she stepped forward to greet her father in the wheelchair. He appeared worn and tired, his once alert, steady gaze dull and lifeless as if he'd lost hope. His features were gaunt, his cheeks sunken, his skin had a gray pallor.

Upon fully seeing his appearance, Saffron's heart ached for her father as her eyes welled with tears. Ruth promised she'd experience everything she saw, heard, and smelled—complete with the accompanying emotional reactions—as if she were still alive. But she'd be unable to offer comfort to those who needed it or speak with anyone other than Amanda.

If I'd only known my father needed me so badly, I would have asked to speak with him instead of Amanda. She may not have been able to solve her murder, but her father needed her and that was more important right now.

Amanda stuck out one hand, which her father ignored, preferring to keep his hands folded in his lap.

He was dressed in a navy-blue tracksuit, his feet covered by slippers that were almost worn through with use. The front of the zippered jacket was covered in soup stains. "Mr. Smythe, it's a pleasure to see you again, sir. How long has it been? Ten years?"

His eyes narrowed. "Do I know you?" he asked, his voice raspy and dry.

Amanda dropped her hand to her side, her smile still bright and inviting. "I'm Amanda Dark. Phillip Swann's friend."

His brow creased in thought for several seconds until he nodded. "Yes, the ghost person. You talk to the dead."

"Yes, sir, I am blessed, or some would say cursed, with that particular gift."

The old man eyed her with one gray eyebrow arched. "My daughter died eight years ago. Are you communicating with her ghost now, is that why you're here?" He snorted bitterly. "And I suppose you want money."

Amanda shook her head. "No, sir, Phillip works for you at the firm and your daughter approached us asking for our help. We won't be billing anything for my services."

Robert Swann shook his head. "She died in a car accident.

Why would she want to talk to me now, after all this time?"

Car accident? thought Saffron. "Amanda, who died in a car accident? I drowned in a bathtub. I remember it."

Amanda nodded to Saffron. "Sir, I thought your daughter drowned."

Robert laughed derisively, his humor tainted with bitterness. "No, no, that's Saffron. That lazy, ungrateful drunk drowned herself after partying all night with her so-called friends. She spent my money recklessly and selfishly. She deserved to die." He paused and hung his head.

"My precious Sadie, she died in the car wreck not a mile from the estate. Her death ended my life's work." A tear escaped his right eye, running down his cheek until it fell off the edge of his bony chin to splash on the foyer floor.

Saffron couldn't believe what she was hearing. If she had been murdered, then either her father had done it or her beloved twin sister had done the deed. She suspected she'd been drugged, then passed out in the bathtub and drowned. An engineered accident covered up by a powerful law firm with friends in high places, including the police department.

"

Amanda," Saffron whispered. "Don't go any further. I don't want to know."

Amanda looked at her with wide eyes. "But it means you won't be able to go to your final destination, ever."

"Are you crazy, woman?" asked Robert, his eyes wild and his cheeks flushed by a surge of anger. "Who are you talking to?"

Amanda turned to face Robert in his wheelchair. "Your daughter, Saffron, is here with me," she said, glaring at him. "And right now, I must explain a few things to her; then you and I must talk. Sir," she added firmly, her hazel eyes now hard, the smile but a memory.

Robert sagged in his chair, his hands fidgeting erratically in his lap, his face twisted by a scowl.

Amanda faced Saffron. "I checked your file at Phillip's office before I came here." She paused and Saffron could see the mix of emotions on her wholesome features. The paranormal detective took in a deep breath to steady herself and then continued. "Yes, you died in the bath. Drowned, as you say. The police investigated after the coroner determined you had an overdose of sleeping pills in your blood stream.

"The investigation resulted in a ruling of accidental overdose, which led to your drowning. Then there was a notation found in your diary—"

"Sadie wrote the suicide note in Saffron's diary," Robert suddenly blurted, his words angry. "I provided the overdose of pills. I killed my own daughter." He steered the wheelchair across the marble floor, right at Amanda, who stepped aside as he stopped. He stuck out a bony index finger at her. "And I'd do it again. Sadie deserved a chance to run the firm. She was a lawyer but their late mother, who controlled the real family money, included a clause in her will that required the firm be sold after my death and the proceeds divided equally between the twins.

"Sadie would have saved *my* firm from extinction. Saffron was a party girl who would have destroyed the firm I built. All she cared about was satisfying her own selfish pleasures. If anything happened to Sadie after I died Saffron would have assumed control of the firm." He sagged in his chair and his voice dropped to a hoarse whisper. "I couldn't le that happen."

"Sadie would have kept up the family tradition. Saffron deserved to die so her sister could inherit the business." He paused when his voice cracked.

Clearing his throat Robert shook his head. "It seemed to make sense then...now that my own days are numbered I'm not so sure."

His watery gaze shifted to Amanda. "I realize now I was wrong. Tell Saffron I'm sorry. I made a mistake." He began to sob, and Saffron sensed his terrible pain and regret.

Amanda looked again at Saffron. "Well, what do you want to do?"

Saffron thought for a few seconds and then made up her mind. "I'm going to stay at Smythe Hall by my father's side until he dies. I still love him and I forgive him."

"You do know you won't be able to change your mind?"

Saffron nodded.

The doorbell rang, interrupting them. Amanda went to the door and pulled the drape aside. Phillip stood at the door. She waved to him, then turned back to face Robert Smythe, who gazed back at her with red-rimmed eyes.

"Mr. Smythe, I'm going to leave you now. I wish you well, sir, but I still feel your daughter has made a poor decision. If I had my way, and there were sufficient evidence, I would go to the police.

But I imagine the extensive cover-up of your crime and the fact it occurred ten years ago make any investigation not worthwhile."

Ignoring Amanda's words, Robert Smythe's eyes reflect his realization that his murdered daughter's spirit was in the room with them. "What did Saffron decide?"

"She's forgiven you and will be staying on as the resident ghost of Smythe Hall." The corners of Amanda's mouth curled up slightly as she shared a knowing look with Saffron. "At least for a while."

Amanda then opened the front door and went outside, closing it with a soft *thump* behind her.

Saffron gazed at her father in his wheelchair, his pale gray eyes fearful, and wondered how long he would live. She would haunt him until then, hopefully helping him to come to grips with what he had done and the consequences he might suffer when his day at the way station came. She wondered where Ruth would assign him. *Probably not the place with the wings.*

One thing she knew for certain; she would see Amanda Dark again, when the time was right.

Clubhouse Heroes

THE AIR IN SPIKE ARNOLD'S FATHER'S garage reeked of sweat and was hotter than the the middle class neighborhood of bungalows and split lelve houses surrounding his parents three bedroom bungalow on Spence Street. My parent's house was two blocks over on Chamberlain Lane. No doubt it wouldn't be any cooler, or warmer for that matter, than Spike's place. But we couldn't meet at my house. My older sister and brother were jerks who treated my friends like they were super annoying cold sores. At least they had the super part right.

Though Mr. Arnold had converted the garage to a workshop the enclosed room still had a slight smell of gasoline and oil.

No doubt the cement floor had absorbed the oil and gas leaks from the cars parked in here since the house was built in the 1950's. At least that's what Spike claimed when one of the guys brought it up at a previous meeting.

But we all knew Mr. Arnold was a lazy butt. He hadn't bothered to fix up the workshop properly. Instead he built it fast and as cheap as possible with a wobbly wooden workbench against one wall constructed from two by fours and a sheet of three quarter inch plywood he ripped off from a construction site. There were six wooden kitchen chairs that creaked when we sat on them he found at the dump. He never built anything in here at least as far as we knew so we used it as our clubhouse.

The truth was the workshop was Mr. Arnold's hide out from Spike's mother who had the reputation as the neighborhood witch. Mrs. Arnold was always angry frequently yelling at us kids for riding our bikes too fast, or screaming at us when we laughed too loud as we walked past her house on the way home from school. Yeah, she's a real piece of work.

Russ Crossley

The garage had its secrets not the least of which was Mr. Arnold's stack of Playboys we boys found in a dusty, rotting cardboard box in one corner, and his stash of empty whiskey bottles behind the water heater in another box with not a drop of booze in them. Believe me we checked each bottle and they were dry. No wonder he didn't get any work done in the garage with all this wonderful soft porn and booze. The guy was only human after all.

Recently we admitted a girl into the club so Playboy's had given way to hair the color of copper, pale cheeks dotted with freckles, and a laugh that made you smile even if you were having a shit day. Too bad she didn't laugh much.

Her name is Izzy—short for Isabelle—Creek. For the first time in my life I fell in love at first sight with this vision of girlhood. This skinny, gangly girl may have a chip on her shoulder the size of the empire state building, but I had fallen hard for her. Every time I saw her at school or at one these weekly meetings my mouth dried and my heart beat faster every time I saw her.

Naturally she had no idea about my feelings, nor had I shared my need to kiss Izzy with the guys. The teasing would have been constant and merciless.

Clubhouse Heroes

In preparation for today's meeting I grabbed a chair from where they were lined up in front of the wall of rakes and shovels and garden hoes standing in the makeshift rack comprised of nails banged into a two by four which was screwed into the wall. The handle of tool was placed between two nails nailed close together so it wouldn't fall over. I set the chair in the center of the cement floor avoiding a large oil stain on the gray cement.

Us guys are thirteen now having grown up in the neighborhood together, played sports together, fought bully's together, went to the movies together, ya know all the guy crap. But now that Izzy had entered our world I sensed things were about to change. Especially since we all had super powers now.

Our health class teacher, Mrs. Isometric, told us puberty would be a bitch (well maybe not those exact words), but she never prepared us for spontaneously developing superpowers after our thirteenth birthdays. Catholic boys and girls have the Sacrament of Confirmation when they come of age. Jewish boys become a bar mitzvah usually at thirteen while Jewish girls become a bat mitzvah at twelve. What the hell do you call a super hero when they mature and gain their powers?

Super charged?

I hadn't told anyone about my powers because I am the largest boy physically in the club at five feet six inches tall with a wide chest and muscular arms and legs sprouting hair already. I'm still a little clumsy. My parents say I had a summer growth spurt which is why I'm so much bigger than the other kids my age, but Im so embarrassed after gym class when we have to use the communal showers.

The real problem though is my *gifts* don't fit my appearance.

I'm able to extend small sticky hairs from the palms of my hands and the soles of my feet using them to climb walls as easily as an insect. I would say the words human fly to describe my talents but it's sooo embarrassing that the biggest guy in the club represents the smallest creature on the planet.

Now me being able to climb walls without ropes or any gear may seem cool, and truthfully by itself it wouldn't be so bad, but there's more. I'm project empathy onto others.

The first time it happened I projected empathy onto my big sister, Maxine—known by her more common moniker, Max—when our cat died.

Clubhouse Heroes

My sister, fifteen going on thirty-five, is a stoned cold bitch with a bad attitude who can burn toast with her eyes. Literally.

I fully expected one day the club would have to fight her since I knew my creep of a sister is going to be a super villain and try to take over the world.

Anyway, as dad carried poor dead Scraps to the car to take him to the vet for disposal Max was being a real rat bag referring to Scraps as a fleabag whose best friends were the filthy mice inhabiting the falling down garden shed in our back yard.

Now this may be true, Scraps had been a lazy cat, but I was still pissed at her so I projected empathy onto her. While her attitude changed immediately, and she went with dad to the vet to drop off the kitty corpse, she returned home with fire in her eyes intending to sizzle my ass like an over done steak.

Somehow she knew what I had done to her.

To escape her death rays I climbed the tallest cedar tree in the heavily wooded green space down the street from our house. She needed time to cool off. Breathing hard the smell of tree sap filling my mouth and nose I knew all I had done was delay our eventual showdown, but like in the movies older sisters eventually forgive their younger siblings, or so I hoped.

Russ Crossley

Spike and I were the only ones to arrive so far for today's meeting. Spike's blond hair was styled in what's known as Liberty Spikes. The name is meant to be synonymous with the Statue of Liberty. The spikes run down from the front center of the head in a straight line to the nape of the neck, the hair on the sides is shaved or cropped so short that the scalp is easily visible. The result looks like a crown similar to the one atop the Statue of Liberty. He'd colored the spiky hair purple. Spike is so awesome.

To complete his super hero persona Spike usually wore a black leather jacket, blue jeans, and leather boots the color of the charcoal briquettes my father burned at in his barbecue grill completing his scary look.

Today was hot so he'd doffed his leathers in favor of a white tee shirt, black shorts, and open toed back plastic sandals on his narrow feet.

Spike's talent is the ability to fly so he can swoop down on people as if he were a giant crow with spikes on his head. He'd even developed a screeching cry to augment his fierce look. Anyone who heard his shrill cry for the first time usually wet themselves, which he really liked and made me laugh. So far his guise as Liberty Spike had worked perfectly.

Clubhouse Heroes

He ran off a few baddies trying to steal old ladies purses outside senior's homes across the city.

Spike had become quite the celeb among the seniors set and they had a hell of a gettin'-the-word-out network amongst the retirement homes around the city to spread the word about his exploits.

In contrast the cops discouraged us saying The Clubhouse Heroes (as the news websites had taken to calling us) were vigilantes who took the law into their own hands. The city should have given the guys medals but the stupid jerks just didn't appreciate our talents and the cops resented them.

The dangerous side of the job stopped Spike and the others for going full on super. None of them were gifted with invulnerability.

Spike caught my eye and grinned before he snagged a chair for himself carried it to the center of the garage setting it next to mine. I could smell the spearmint gum on his breath as he walked past me. "You're early, comic book," he said as he plunked himself down on the chair causing it to creak in the still, warm air.

My real name is Bobby Strang but the guys call me comic book because I collect super hero comics.

I am the club consultant since I had an extensive collection of super hero comics going back to when I was five years old and my dad bought me my first one at a drug store. I'd been collecting comic books ever since.

The thought crossed my mind to call Spike Captain Obvious, but the side door leading to the walkway to the front door of the house burst open interrupting me before I could speak. The sound of familiar laughter wafted through the open door.

Ach, Izzy, and Mark had arrived. Besides it made no sense to piss off Spike as the keeper of the keys to our clubhouse.

When someone in the club discovered my collecting hobby on my Front Book page they asked me to join. I jumped at the chance to work with actual super heroes, it's a fantasy come true for me. None of the guys ever told me who spotted my page but I knew it had to be Mark. He reads minds, which is really cool in my opinion, but he says it's not all that great to read minds especially at school. Eighth grade politics can tear you up, man.

Mark Fasberg is black with thick short curls covering his nearly perfect round head. He wears wire-rimmed glasses and is of medium build.

Clubhouse Heroes

Not overly muscular he plays left wing midfielder on the school soccer team so he's in pretty good shape.

Then there's Achmed Mahod (we call him Ach for short) whose family emigratted from Syria to the U.S. in the '70's. His special gift is his ability shoot water from his fingers that he can direct at any object or person he chooses. I don't know how he does this without drying up like the riverbed out near the old gravel pit, but he's great to have around on a camping trip when you need to extinguish the campfire. It saves your arms and hands from having to lug water in buckets for a stream or lake.

Of course the question we get asked all the time is do the guys, and Izzy, plan to use their gifts for good or evil. Since they don't know how to respond to this question they tell reporters and neighbors and our parents they have no idea explaining they're just kids. While the adults seem to accept this lame answer to what I think is very serious question I'm certain they're afraid they might end up on the dark side of the coin.

Knowing comic books like I do I'm not so sure myself.

These guys, and Izzy, have strong personalities and insecurities abound given we are pre-teens and uncertain where our lives are headed at the moment.

Speaking for myself I'm determined to be a good guy, not a villain.

"Hey, comic book," says Mark grabbing another chair from the ones left near the wall of tools. He grinned at me.

I nodded. "Hey, Mark, Ach, Izzy...good to see you guys..." My cheeks suddnely felt warm as I realized I had called Izzy a guy. She however didn't seem to notice my mistake her eyes cast downward as she grabbed a vacant chair and dragged it noisily across the cement floor until it was next one of the others we were setting up in a semicircle.

"Hey, Izzy," protested Spike, "my dad's gonna freak if you break that." He nodded at the chair. She smirked at him her eyes narrowing to slits and sat down with her arms crossed over her chest. She wore jean shorts and a bulky gray sweatshirt with a hood. On her feet were pink flip-flops.

"Let's get on with this. I got stuff to do," she said, her tone registering her annoyance.

Clubhouse Heroes

Everyone including me sat down. I studied the features of the members of our little band of would be heroes each in turn. None of them looked particularly pleased to be here as if they had better things to do. Not that I blamed them they probably did. Most kids are over scheduled by their parents in some mistaken belief this will build character and lead to success in life. Like me these kids were ignored by their parents and were social outcasts in the pressure cooker known as high school.

In contrast to the others Mark was smiling and looked pleased with himself about something he'd no doubt learned when he read a mind. I wasn't going to be the first one to ask in case he had read mine and learned of my infatuation with the female in our midst. Mind readers are incredibly nosy about other peoples business.

Since the clubhouse was in Spike's garage he acted as chair for the meetings. Pulling out his cell phone to glance at the screen he nodded and emitted a soft grunt. "Okay, guys, it's 10 a.m. Saturday morning, July 3rd. tomorrow is the 4th of July."

Again with the Captain Obvious stuff. What was up with him? Was he trying to annoy us on purpose?

Izzy and Ach seemed fixated on the oil stain on the garage floor their expression blank and their eyes reflecting their lack of interest.

Spike's brow wrinkled and he glared at Mark. "What's so funny, bud?"

Mark chuckled generating stares from Ach and Izzy. At least they had finally joined the rest of us. "We finally have soemthing we can do," said Mark.

I swallowed hard. Did he know about my secret ability?

"What?" said Spike clearly annoyed.

"There is going to be an attack at the picnic tomorrow in Grammer Park. We will stop it and catch the criminals who want to disrupt the picnic."

Izzy grunted. "What a load of shit, Mark. How do you know there's going to be an attack? And who are the criminals?"

Mark leaned back in the chair stretching his long legs out crossing his ankles and his arms. "I often walk or ride my bike around the neighborhood reading a few minds randomly. Yesterday I read the minds of the plotters. A girl and a guy."

"Where?" I blurted without thinking. This could be my chance to reveal myself to the club to make a real contribution. Braised I really was interested.

Clubhouse Heroes

Ever since I'd learned of Mark's gift I'd wanted to be able to read minds. It must be awesome to hear other's people's thoughts in your head.

I froze when I realized all eyes were on me. I shrugged and offered a weak chuckle. "I mean what house or was it on the street? It'll help us find them."

Spike's mouth formed a sneer. "Comic book," he began with that voice my dad reserved for those times when I screwed up. My stomach tightened and anger rose in my throat. I really hate that voice.

"You won't be coming on the mission with us. We're the super powered heroes, all you do is provide stuff about what super heroes can do and not do." His eyes shot to Izzy then back to me. His lean frame relaxed. "Besides you might get hurt and we can't let that happen." He shrugged. "You're a member of the club," Spike added as if this explained everything.

They were blowing me off. They didn't respect me or the intelligence gathering I'd contributed to the club so far.

Spike directed his attention to Mark whose smile had faded. "Who are these criminals?"

Mark shrugged. "I'm not exactly sure because they're using super villain names. The girl is called Burnout and the guy is Projectile.

She can burn stuff with her eyes; he shoots steel darts from devices strapped to the underside of his wrists. According to my reads (mark calls his mind reading *reads*) he made the devices after stealing the designs for the technology from a DOD computer system he hacked."

Izzy's eyes widened. "Military hardware?"

Matt nodded matter of factly. "Yeah. Experimental stuff."

"What are they planning?"

Matt's brow wrinkled and his eyes narrowed. "I'm not sure exactly only that it has something to do with the 4th of July party at the park."

Spike rose to his feet and walked to a blue plastic bin overflowing with newspapers and advertising flyers. I thought about helping him but remained seated when the others didn't offer. I'm a bit of a follower that way. I volunteered once for hallway monitor in elementary school and got beat up after school almost every day until I quit. Following the group was better than being the punching bag of the week.

While Spike shuffled through the stack of old newspapers Izzy stood up and went to the old fridge in one corner of the garage where Spike's mom kept a supply of soda in various flavors.

Clubhouse Heroes

"Wan' one?" she said glancing over her shoulder at us before she opened the fridge door.

"Grape," said Mark. I asked for an orange. Ach wanted a diet cola. She brought back three cans including her fav, lemon lime. She tossed us our sodas then sat once again on the chair next to Ach. I secretly would have preferred her next to me, but this wasn't the right time. Some days I wondered if the right time would ever come.

"Aha," said Spike holding a newspaper triumphantly in his right hand.

Staring at Spike I pulled the aluminum tab to open the can of cold soda and took a long drink then said, (after first letting an orange flavored burp pass my lips) "Okay, what's the deal?"

Spike brought the newspaper over and dropped it on the seat of his empty chair. "Look at the headline." I leaned forward as did Izzy and Ach. I shared a look of horror with them after we scanned the large block lettering across the front page of the town paper. It read, MAYOR INVITES VICE PRESIDENT TO ATTEND JULY 4TH PICNIC.

Oh. My. American Idol.

***

After begging and pleading—I texted Mark, Spike, and Ach every ten minutes for the rest of the day until they agreed I should some—I convinced the guys to let me join the club at the park. Not that they could stop me, since this is a public event and I'm still part of the public.

What disappointed me the most was Izzy's attitude. She didn't seem to care if I came along or not. It was actually Mark who seemed to be the only one concerned about my safety.

Anyway, when we arrived at the park the place was jammed with people, their kids and dogs running wild all over the tramped down grass which probably would be dead until next spring. Not that this was my problem, but I enjoy green grass and the smell when it's fresh cut. All right I'm weird, what can I say?

There were families sitting on blankets or law chairs covering the park with an elevated platform containing a band consisting of three guys with guitars, a guy beating on some drums, and a girl who was the lead singer. When we arrived the band had just started playing old Beatle tunes. (My mom irons our clothes with the radio tuned to the oldies station.).

Clubhouse Heroes

Under the branches of a stand of firs and oak trees beyond the picnickers was a row of gas barbecues cooking burgers, hot dogs, ribs, and polish sausages. My stomach grumbled when the smell of the grease and charred meat wafted over us. I only had a bowl of Toasty Oaties before heading for the park this morning so I was hungry.

"Strangely inappropriate that they're playing songs by a British rock group on the day we celebrate our independence from the Brits don't ya think?" murmured Izzy. I choked back a laugh and she glanced at me with a brief smile on her lips.

Surveying the chaos on this sunny day the sun beating down on us from a cloudless azure sky I didn't see anyone that could be described as a super villain. But they might not be dressed like the villains in the comic books. If they were smart they'd be dressed as if they were picnickers enjoying the day.

A guy dressed as a clown with a red nose, white face and blue hair wearing a baggy blue and green stripped one piece suit walked past me accompanied by someone dressed as Uncle Sam with a wig of white hair and a goatee wearing a red and white striped top hat with white stars on a blue band, a blue tail coat, and red and white striped pants.

Looking at their feet as they walked away from me I noticed something strange about them. They were wearing boots; work boots like construction crews wear on job sites. The day was hot and humid so wearing costumes would be uncomfortable enough so what gives with the work boots?

I moved to stand beside Mark who was focused on the barbecues in the distance a trickle of drool seeping from one side of his mouth. He was hungry too. You know what they say, breakfast of champions...or some such crap.

"Hey, Mark, do a read of those two." I indicated the clown and the Uncle Sam who appeared to be headed in the direction of the stage where no doubt the Veep and the mayor would be making their speeches. I really hate speeches because they're dull as the polish on my Sunday-go-ta-meetin' shoes, but I don't think anyone needs to be killed for making them, no doubt some people would disagree.

Mark looked at them and went silent. His eyes narrowed slightly. This was the only outward sign he was conducting a read of others people's minds which made him the perfect spy. If he weren't a decent guy I would have been worried he'd use his gift for bad stuff.

Izzy appeared on edge she was shuffling her feet while Ach was pretending to watch the baseball game going on at the ball field to out left. Spike had already taken off and was flying across the line of trees trying to avoid anyone seeing him. He was keeping under the shade of the branches and was dressed all in black so unless someone knew where to look they probably wouldn't see him. That was until we had to take action.

All around us were happy kids and teenagers their voices buzzing with shouts and laughter. Everyone was having fun except us.

My gut was tight with tension and I fixed my eyes on the retreating clown and Sam. Finally Mark spoke. "They're the ones alright." His tone was grim which is unusual for a happy go lucky guy like him. Mark shifted his gaze to me. "What are we gonna do?"

I had no idea realizing we hadn't taken the time to plan anything. I cringed inside. What lame ass heroes we turned out to be. How did we not think to plan something when we found the villains? Of course I don't think we ever truly believed we'd find them.

Not that we doubted Mark's abilities but until now he'd been good at finding lost keys and reading the answers for tests at school in the minds of the smart kids, ya know the ones who studied every night. Uncovering an evil plot to kill the vice president of the United States seemed a little far fetched even to me the comic book guy.

I shook my head. "I'm not sure," I said, my words sounded weak even to me.

"Well, we have to do something," chimed in Izzy.

Shifting to look at her I saw her lean body had tensed and her hand had formed fists at her sides. She still wore jean shorts with a fresh sleeveless forest green top, and she had doffed her preferred flip-flops the color of bubble gum in favor of black and gray tennis shoes. Running around a park battling super villains wearing flips flops didn't seem dignified or practical.

I knew she was right of course. I decided then I would take the direct approach. I set off after the clown and Sam moving quickly through the crowd of happy picnickers. Men holding beer cans, ladies in tube tops sunning themselves laying in blankets on the grass, children tossing balls, or playing tag their faces sticky with blue or pink cotton candy.

I dodged them all until I finally caught up with the villains who were nearing the band platform where the speeches were scheduled.

"Hey!" I shouted at the clown who didn't turn at the sound of my voice. Suddenly a large muscular body slammed into my side knocking the wind out of me and causing me to fall onto the grass.

Stars danced across my vision and I gasped for breath my side aching from the impact. A heavy weight pressed down on me pinning me to the ground.

"Hey!" I heard Izzy shout. "What the hell are you doing to my friend?"

The weight eased off me then disappeared as I managed to sit up coughing and sucking in air. My vision cleared and I saw a large man in a dark blue business suit standing over me his dark eyes glaring at me. "Secret service, ma'am," he said pulling a small black wallet from his inside suit pocket. He flashed a badge at identification card at me then put it back in his pocket.

"Why did you tackle him?" said Izzy her tone angry.

The man's already beady eyes narrowed. "I'm with the Vice President's protection detail and your *friend* was about to attack—" He stopped talking and his tanned cheeks flushed crimson. "Move along."

He started to walk away when he stopped and glanced back at us. "And don't come back." He hurried away and soon disappeared into the crowd.

I looked at Mark. "Is he for real?" I croaked in a harsh whisper.

Mark shrugged his expression sheepish. "Yeah, he's who he says he is. He was protecting the Uncle Sam. As I read it they caught Projectile and have an undercover agent infiltrating by wearing the get up he planned to use to get close to the Veep."

"So the Sam isn't a villain?" asked Izzy her eyes wide. Mark nodded. Izzy grunted. "How about the clown?"

He nodded. "Oh, yeah she's a super villain alright. She's comic books sister."

My heart skipped a beat. Max a super villain? Sure she's a real bitch on wheels but a super villain? "No way," I said. You must be wrong."

Mark pointed an index finger at the side of his head. "I might be but this is never wrong." Ach rolled his eyes. I was beginning to doubt him.

Suddenly a large black shadow swooped over us from above. Spike had returned from his spying. He landed next to me as Mark held out a hand to help me stand. My breathing had returned to normal.

"Why don't we just tell the secret service guy about the clown and let them take care of it."

"And let her kill them too?" I said. I'd seen my sister in action. She would burn them to ash before they could stop her.

"Why's the Veep coming to the picnic if there's an chance a super villain will try to kill him?" asked Izzy. It was a good question that none of us had the answer to. I could have asked the secret service guy if I could find him and he wouldn't kick my butt.

I knew then what we had to do.

An hour later with the arrival of the Veep's motorcade we had donned our disguises. We were disguised as clowns and stood behind the rope barriers set up to make a path fro the vice president and mayor to make their way to the stage. The secret service comprised of men and women in dark suits sunglasses covering their eyes flanked the stretch limo.

One agent opened the rear door and the Veep got out while the portly mayor exited the car on the other side. Man, is he fat.

The crowd of picnickers had lined up on both sides of the ropes to watch. They cheered as the Veep waved and smiled at the crowd.

Russ Crossley

She was prettier in person than on TV. Her blonde curls brushed the shoulders of her tanned suit jacket.

The mayor joined her standing to her left smiling with obvious pride as she greeted the crowd with obvious enthusiasm. Clearly she wasn't afraid of any super villains that might be lurking around.

Suddenly the clown we'd seen earlier burst through the crowd knocking over people like bowling pins until she leapt over a small boy to land on the makeshift pathway as if she were a cat facing the startled vice president. A female secret service agent stepped in front of the vice president as flames shot from the clowns eyes to engulf the agent in orange and red flames. She screamed as shouts of horror and fear erupted in the crowd.

Then, as if someone had fired a starter pistol at a big race, the picnickers scattered wildly running in all directions. Children screamed and shouts to look out holy mother of god help he's burning echoed chaotically over the park. A perfect 4th of July had suddenly become an orgy of panic, death and pain.

Ach shot water out of his fingers quickly dousing the flames on the secret service agent who had collapsed into a heap.

Simultaneously Spike had leapt into the air and landed hard on the deadly clown knocking her to the ground. He punched her in the face aiming in particular for the eyes hoping to stop her from setting him on fire too.

He kept punching until realizing he might kill her I moved to stop him grabbing his arm, as he was about to throw another punch. The makeup had fallen off her face and I saw my sister was unconscious, bruises already beginning to appear on her cheeks. Her eyes were swollen.

"Spike, take it easy. You don't want to kill her do ya?"

Spike looked at me his eyes blazing with fury. "Don't I?"

I patted his shoulder and he visible relaxed then climbed off my sister's prone form. We all wanted to avenge the brutal murder of the agent.

I glanced at the limo and saw the vice president inside her eyes wide before the tires screeched and the car drove away at high speed. I saw the mayor lying on his back next to the car with a first aid attendant pressing hard on his chest. I discovered later he'd had a heart attack. He was declared dead on arrival at the hospital.

Distant sirens began to fill the air getting louder with each passing second. I looked around at the clubhouse heroes, Izzy, Ach, Mark, and Spike. They were in shock but we had done our job. We stopped an assassination.

"Let's head for the clubhouse," I said softly.

They nodded in unison and we started to walk away trying not to be noticed. We dropped out clown disguises as we walked. No doubt the cops would be interested in anyone dressed as a clown for some time to come.

"What about your sister?" asked Izzy.

I looked back at my unconscious sister still lying on the trampled grass. I had no idea what would happen to her only that she would go to jail for a long time. I projected empathy toward her and hoped this time it would stick.

I stopped to gaze into Izzy's eyes. "I have something to tell you," I said.

Her eyes grew wider as I revealed my secret gifts to her and the others. They didn't tease me; in fact they welcomed me into the clubhouse heroes.

Sure our first mission had been successful but even success has a price.

It's A Small Galaxy

SHEILA CULPEPPER YAWNED as she shuffled across the cool ceramic tiles on the kitchen floor toward the door to the pantry. The kitchen cupboard where they kept her favorite full-fiber breakfast cereal was again empty.

Her grey eyes drifted toward Bernie, her husband of fifteen years, sitting on a burnished steel stool, topped with a crimson, mushroom-shaped cushion, his narrow shoulders hunched over as he read the morning news on the virtual screen hovering over the speckled granite island. A half-eaten bowl of her cereal floating in a bath of almond milk sat untouched on the island to his left. She rolled her eyes. He wasted more than he ate.

Will Bernie ever remember to restock the cupboards or will I be doing this for the rest of my days? she wondered.

Her attention shifted to the cupboard door.

"Open," she said, pulling her robe tighter about her narrow waist.

The door slide aside and she froze. Was she seeing things? She pinched her arm and it hurt, so she wasn't dreaming. She eyed the thing blocking the shelf of cereal, rice, and dried pasta. *What the hell is this?*

Inside the pantry was a tall creature—no other words came to mind to describe it—covered head to toe in matted brown hair. It's inky gaze was unfocussed and its mouth hung open, revealing razor sharp teeth both top and bottom of the snout-like jaw. It didn't appear to be wearing clothing; the hair covering its body obscured any anatomical details.

She shot Bernie a disparaging look over her left shoulder. "Bernie," she said between gritted teeth, her tone sharp as a new shaving razor.

He either didn't hear her or was ignoring her on purpose, his eyes still narrow and focused on what she could make out from across the island was an article on celestial mechanics as they related to the new interstellar propulsion system being developed by GenY Astro Nav Corporation.

Him and his damned engines.

It's A Small Galaxy

She'd always wondered why the most gifted, award-winning bioengineer in the galaxy wasted his free time studying rocket jockey crap. All he ever said was he liked to tinker with engines. Her man-dar told her his explanations were evasive, but his love of rockets was the one part of his life he refused to share with her. At least until the hair suit giant showed up the cupboard. Now Bernie had two secrets and she didn't like it one bit.

"Bernie!"

Though she hated raising her voice, she'd finally gained his attention. He looked at her, his mouth hanging open, his azure eyes wide registering a look of surprise dusted with a modicum of impatience. His black curled hair was askew, looking as if it had been pressed to one side on his oval head. He was dressed in a slate gray, short-sleeved tee shirt and matching sports shorts—his usual bedtime attire.

"What?" he said. "I'm busy. I—" He stopped short, his mouth hanging open when he noticed the reddish hue born of anger on Sheila's face, and her fiery glare.

Sheila stepped aside to reveal the huge hairy beast in the pantry behind her—she decided to try out different descriptions to see how they sounded.

Unfortunately, beast didn't sound as good a description as creature; it didn't seem to fit. Creature seemed more apropos.

His face flushed the colour of the stoplight at the corner of oh-oh and aw, crap. "Uhhh...listen, Sheila. I'm sorry. I should have told you..." His words petered out.

"Did your father drop this *thing* off?" (Thing seemed a worthy contender for a description.)

Bernie nodded.

"When?"

Bernie's father, Jules, was always bringing over some piece of crap (Jules and Bernie called them treasures, she called them crap) he discovered at flea markets and yard sales.

"Yesterday."

"Well, what is it and what are we supposed to do with it?"

Bernie instructed the virtual screen to turn off, climbed off the stool, and walked to her, his bare feet padding in the quiet kitchen. As he reached her, then gripped the sides of her shoulders and gazed into her eyes, his look said something she hadn't seen before. Her heart went out to her beloved husband. She hated to see him in pain.

"What's wrong?" she asked, her voice barely above a whisper.

"My dad's terminally ill and he's decided to let a few things go before..." His words caught in his throat and his eyes welled with tears. Shelia stepped up and enveloped him in her arms. He shuddered as a sob escaped his lips.

She could feel his heart beating faster and the warmth of him, and the remnants of his aftershave from yesterday filled her nostrils, the odor reminding her of the beach where they used to go for family picnics with Jules when their kids were little. A deep sense of sadness fell over her. She'd lost her own parents in a car crash before the fully-automated driver control system had been developed; now she would be losing Jules, too.

Bernie's mother had died during a deep space research mission years ago when Bernie was in his late teens. Jules had lived alone for the past seventy years.

Shaking off the feelings caused by the memories that had surfaced, she realized she didn't recall seeing a giant, hair-covered creature in Jules garage or anywhere in his three-bedroom bungalow in West Vancouver. Given the size of the thing, it would have been hard to miss.

Finally she released Bernie and took a step back to gaze into his teary eyes. "I'm so sorry about Jules," she said in a low voice. "But it still doesn't explain the big hair-ball in our pantry."

Bernie's chin slumped to his chest. "Dad once brought home a science kit as a present when he returned from an off world business trip. I was ten."

"I don't understand," Sheila said.

"The kit was an alien bioengineering toy designed for their children to learn how to make clones."

Sheila's eyes went wide and her heart beat faster as the implications of what her husband was saying sank in. "You mean you made a *real* Sasquatch?"

Bernie wiped his eyes with the back of one hand and nodded sheepishly. "I named him Shakespeare... and I referred to him as a Bigfoot rather than the more correct first nations name." He avoided her by looking out the sliding glass door overlooking the sunshine-soaked pool in the backyard. He shrugged. "To a ten-year-old, Bigfoot sounds cooler than Sasquatch."

Sheila shook her head in wonder. She thought for a second, then realized something important. "But no one's ever found a living Bigfoot or Sasquatch... whatever." This conversation was fast sinking into the ridiculous zone.

Bernie shifted to look at her, his eyes reflecting growing excitement. If this had been one of his deep secrets, he certainly appeared happy to share it now. "That's the big thing about this...uh, *toy* I made. I used DNA extracted from Bigfoot droppings from the Sasquatch museum near Squamish."

"Okay, so Shakespeare is a toy and your dad kept him to gather dust until, now, he's dropped it off for you." Sheila pondered her words for a moment. "What are we going to do with it?"

"With what?" said a voice from the entryway into the kitchen. It was Ryder, their eleven-year-old son. He entered, still dressed in his navy-blue shorts and white tee shirt, his narrow feet encased in his favourite fuzzy slippers.

Sheila turned toward her son and smiled. "Morning, Ryder, how'd you sleep?"

The towheaded boy, his pale green eyes roaming the room, padded across the tiled floor until he suddenly froze and his eyes became wide as saucers, staring openmouthed at the tall, hairy creature inside the open pantry.

"What is that?" he asked, his voice filled with wonder. Clearly, he wasn't afraid. His eyes relaxed and he started forward, but before he got too close, Sheila grabbed his arm and restrained him.

She was still unsure if the beast (*maybe beast was a good word*?) was dangerous. It may have been Bernie's toy when he was a boy, but the creature was massive and those razor-sharp teeth could probably rip flesh from bones.

Bernie chuckled, surprising her. She looked at her husband. He wore a wide smile on his angular features and his right hand covered his mouth.

"What's so funny?" she asked. "Your toy could be dangerous to small children."

Bernie laughed. "Don't be ridiculous, Sheila. Shakespeare's been in stasis for over forty years."

"His name's Shakespeare?'" interrupted Ryder.

Bernie moved to stand beside Ryder and draped one long arm across his son's shoulders, curling his hand around Ryder's other arm, hugging him closer. "Yes, Ry, he's a Bigfoot. He was my favourite toy when I was about your age."

"Where did he come from? And why haven't we seen him before?"

Bernie grinned in obvious pride. "I made him. And Grandpa needed to clear our a few things so he woke him up."

Ryder looked up at his father and frowned as one eyebrow arched on his forehead. "Com'on, Dad, you're kiddin' me, right?"

Bernie chuckled. "No, son, not at all. Grandpa gave me a science kit from another planet and I used it to clone him."

Ryder shrugged. "Okay...I guess..."

Sheila saw the doubt in Ryder's eyes and smiled to herself. Ryder was the brightest kid in his pre-med class and it took a lot, even for a genius like her husband, to put one over on their son.

"Anyone gonna ask me?" The voice was deep and loud in the confines of the pantry cupboard. Slowly Sheila turned to face the creature...the word *monster* suddenly popped into her mind. *Monster...perfect.*

Bernie released Ryder and entered the pantry cupboard. "Hey, Shakespeare, no see long time."
The monster laughed, sounding more like a roaring, ravenous lion than a cryptid creation of her husband's manufacture.

Sheila's heart beat more rapidly, and for the first time since seeing the monster in the pantry (*Hey, not a bad title for my next article*), she worried they might be in danger.

But she relaxed when she saw the monster had wrapped its long arms around her husband's slim body and lifted him off his feet in a bear hug.

The sounds of what was obviously two old friends laughing and muttering unintelligible words of friendship made Sheila feel a little left out.

"Hey, you two," she called, "get a room." She crossed her arms over her chest.

Out of the corner of one eye, she saw Ryder had walked to the cupboard where the cereal was stored where he, too, discovered it was empty. Her stomach growled to remind her she hadn't eaten breakfast yet.

"Listen, Bernie and...."

"Shakespeare," said the monster, his round, beady eyes gazing at her from above Bernie's head. At least she now had a way to measure the size of him. Bernie was almost two meters tall and the creature towered over him, so she realized he had to be at least two and half meters tall.

She offered him a tight smile. She wasn't about to become fast friends with this creature until she knew more about him, and more about his relationship with her husband. Right now, she knew nothing about him.

***

It's A Small Galaxy

After Sheila and Ryder had finished breakfast, they joined Bernie and Shakespeare in the living room, where they had retreated while she and her son ate.

Two boxes of cereal were missing from the pantry shelf, so she assumed the creature—she reminded herself she better use the name Bernie had given the Bigfoot or risk embarrassing herself or Bernie. Truthfully, she didn't care about the monster's feelings. She didn't even know if he had feelings, at least as a human being might understand them.

In the past two hundred years since trade with alien worlds had become more widespread, she had met all sorts of aliens with manners ranging from indifference toward humans to rude to overly— almost intrusively so—friendly; so until she had more time to know him (assuming it really was a *him*), Shakespeare would have to prove himself to her.

Bernie was far too enamoured with his childhood plaything to be honest with her or with himself about the creature. As far as she was concerned, her primary duty was protecting her son. But even Ryder appeared to have become infatuated with Shakespeare. Sheila had to tell him three times not to wolf down his breakfast as if he were a wild animal.

He was so excited by the sudden appearance of the two-and-a-half-meter-tall Bigfoot.

After breakfast the boy tore into the living room ahead of her to join the Bigfoot and his father. Rolling her eyes, she walked to the front room feeling edgy, with butterflies definitely not flying in formation in her stomach. She didn't know why Shakespeare made her nervous but he did.

She found the Bigfoot sitting on the pink and mint-green couch, the cushion mashed flat from his weight—which had to be considerable given his size—and Bernie sat in one of the matching big wing chairs bracketing the couch, laughing. Ryder sat next to Shakespeare. The creature had one hand the size of a baseball glove wrapped around her son's shoulder, hugging him in to his hairy side. The boy's youthful features were split by a wide smile and his inner joy had traveled to his eyes.

Sheila moved across the room and sat on the other wing chair. She watched her son and smiled to herself. He was enjoying meeting his father's childhood toy and listening to their tales of those days. She froze when she heard Shakespeare say something about detectives and it clearly wasn't fictional sleuths.

Bernie had talked about wanting to be a detective as long as she'd known him.

It's A Small Galaxy

All those cheesy ancient stories he read from the net library on his virtual reader about crime and detectives, and those old films he watched every Saturday even when they were dating twenty years ago. She always thought it was his boyhood fantasies. Now here was this childhood toy monster talking about detectives.

"Excuse me, Bernie and...uhhh...Shakespeare. I have a question?" Sheila said, causing three sets of eyes to turn in her direction, including two inky eyes surrounded by bushy hair the colour of her ginger cat. "Ummm...what's this about detectives?"

Shakespeare exchanged a look with Bernie, then the creature began to explain. "After Bernie made me and I had grown to the equivalent of a human teenager, about two years—" Sheila's expression must have been sceptical because the creature stopped to clarify. "Bigfoot's," the creature paused and his snout wrinkled, "or is it Bigfeet?" Shakespeare shook his head. "Anyway, when I was a teenager, Bernie and I decided to become detectives and solve crimes. Ya know, missing pets, break-ins, thefts from backyards. Relatively minor stuff. We didn't want any money for helping out our neighbors, it was purely problem solving. Ya know, fun." Shakespeare laughed in his growly voice.

Russ Crossley

Bernie's eyes became serious. Sheila's body tensed as a knot formed in her stomach. Her husband rarely showed his serious side at home. It kind of turned her on.

Shakespeare continued. "That was until an old man in the neighborhood went missing. We didn't get involved until the police and the neighborhood had conducted a thorough search for him and then eventually called it off."

"What's his name?" asked Ryder.

Shakespeare hugged the boy closer to him. "Min Bakster."

Ryder's brow wrinkled and his eyes became curious. "That's a funny name."

Shakespeare chuckled. "I didn't buy the story myself and tried to convince Bernie it was a neighborhood kid pulling our legs." He cleared his nose with a loud *whuff*, startling Sheila. The sounds coming out of this creature were *so* loud.

Oddly, Ryder and Bernie seemed unfazed. Of course, they often attended the indoor sky car races and the cars' engines were loud, so higher than normal decibel levels didn't bother them. Sheila saw no point to watching sky cars going round and round, but she had her own hobbies they didn't care much about.

Sewing flags, gardening, and water filtration engineering were what she enjoyed.

But, seeing the look of pure joy on her son's features and the twinkle in his eyes, she decided to play along with this ridiculous story. Shakespears brow wrinkled and he seemed deep in thought. "Why don't we ask Min Bakster if he knows where the Cruz kid is now?"

Bernie shrugged. "It's been over forty years...he may have moved away or something. I haven't lived in the old neighbourhood for decades..."

"But, Dad, isn't your parents' house under water?" asked Ryder, his excitement bubbling over in his voice.

Bernie cast Ryder a wry smile. "Yeah, you're right, of course, Ryder. Richmond is under sixteen meters of ocean. We could look for Bakster on the net."

Shakespeare stood, towering over them. "Great idea. Let's find out where Old Man Bakster is now. " He moved to the big screen on the wall over the ice stone fireplace, apparently looking for the *on* button or the remote. No one used such old technology anymore, but he had been in stasis for forty years. Sheila understood immediately and decided to help the poor creature.

Being out of the familiar could be quite unsettling.

She stood and walked to stand beside the mountain of ginger hair. "Things have changed since you went into the deep freeze, Shakespeare." She patted his arm. Surprisingly, his fur was soft to the touch. "Screen on. Net," she said, facing the wide screen.

The digital screen came on with the Peach search engine prominent in the middle of the one hundred and fifty-two centimeter screen. She looked up at Shakespeare, who smiled down at her, his chocolate brown eyes bright. She felt herself warming to this childhood toy of Bernie's, beginning to like the big guy. "Locate Min Bakster."

The search engine began to glow, then an address, contact link number, and picture of Min Bakster appeared. He didn't look as old as Shakespeare and Bernie had suggested. Bakster couldn't be a day over a hundred and thirty-five. "A youngin'," she muttered under her breath.

Sheila turned her head to gaze at Bernie. "Old man? Really?"

Bernie shrugged sheepishly in response.

She chuckled. "Connect with the Bakster link," she said, turning her attention back to the screen.

There was a soft buzz, then the Min Bakster in the picture on his ID file appeared on the screen. Sheila actually thought he looked younger than the digital picture on file. Not surprising with all the regeneration techniques improving every day, it seemed.

Bakster was dressed in a mint-green, short-sleeved dress shirt, his steel gray hair cut short, his azure eyes alert, the corners slightly crinkled. He wore a half smile on his thin, pale lips.

"Yes? Can I help you?" he asked, obviously curious. His eyes briefly widened when his blue-green gaze shifted to the Bigfoot standing beside her, but he didn't seem all that startled by Shakespeare's appearance. Alien contact really had made everyone so blasé these days about seeing odd beings, which a few centuries ago would have brought out the military with guns a blazing.

Good thing, too, she thought. The early days of first contact had not been pretty.

"Hello, Min Bakster," she began, "I'm Sheila Culpepper, and this is Shakespeare. This is going to sound odd, but forty years ago my husband Bernie Culpepper and Shake—"

"Yes, I know who they are," Bakster said, interrupting her.

His brow wrinkled in a frown and his eyes narrowed. His lips formed a grim line. "They caused me all sorts of trouble."

He looked as if he was about to cut the connection, but Sheila needed more information if they were going to solve this mystery. Bernie could be focused to the point of obsession. Even after all these decades, no doubt this problem had been haunting him. Now, with the mystery rekindled, he would become impossible to live with.

"I'm sorry, Min Bakster, but I need to know if you recall another boy in the old neighborhood named Cruz."

His features became hard and his jawline tightened.

"Listen," she said, speaking softly. "I am really sorry if the boys upset you, but I really need to talk to this Cruz person."

Bakster's features relaxed slightly. Sheila knew she could charm even the most hardened curmudgeon; it appeared that included Bakster. *It's a gift.*

"Sorry if I'm being difficult, Sheila Culpepper, but Bernie and Shakespeare put up posters all over town saying I was missing." His features squished up as if he'd sucked on a sour lemon.

"They described me as *old.* I've spent plenty on rejuvenation over the years just to be called *old*?" His scowl deepened. "It was humiliating."

Sheila wanted to laugh but managed to hold back by changing the subject. "Please call me Sheila.... May I call you Min?" He nodded. "Okay, Min, if you tell me where Cruz is, I can clear all this up." She shifted her gaze to Bernie, whose face was red as beet soup. "And I'll make sure Bernie sends you a written apology for his youthful exuberance."

Bernie nodded sheepishly.

Min nodded. "Good, it's about time. You'll find Cruz..."

Sheila's heart began to beat rapidly when Min told them where to find Cruz. She looked up at Shakespeare, who had a wide grin on his furry face.

"Cool!" said Ryder.

***

Sheila stood beside Bernie, with Ryder holding her husband's hand. They stood in front of the viewing window overlooking the large, open launch area where six orbital shuttle pods were being prepared for liftoff. One ivory-white shuttle pod in particular had their attention.

Bernie's father was secured ion the stasis pod where Shakespeare had been kept for forty years. It would keep him alive until the doctors on Shakespear's woeld could save his life with their advanced medical knowledge.

The craft had twin antigravity engine exhausts extending from the rear of the passenger compartment. The short wings had been extended from the bottom of the craft, hiding the tripod landing skids, to aid in stability while the shuttle was still in the atmosphere. The two pilots were visible in windows of the command deck at the front of the pod, their attention focused on final checks before liftoff. Liftoff was set for ten minutes from now.

The shuttle pod would rendezvous with the deep space freighter headed for Shakespeare's races planet in less than an hour. Then the childhood toy Bernie had created would be gone. Though he was created on Earth he really wanted to visit the planet where his race originated. How could Bernie deny him?

"You okay?" Sheila asked, seeing the wistful expression on her husband's face.

"Yeah. I'm fine...I guess. I'm gonna miss him."

Sheila chuckled. "I know, but you haven't seen him in decades; and if what he says is true, he's going to save your father's life on his home world.

Shakespeare's people know more about genetics than any race in the galaxy. They know how to save Dad's life.

"Given the distance to his world, I don't think you'll see Shakespeare again; but your dad will be back in fifty years or so."

Bernie turned to gaze into her eyes. "I owe this all to Bel Cruz. and Min of course. I'd say they're pretty good guys."

Ryder laughed. "Good thing Bel's a star pilot. He knew where Shakespeare's home planet is as soon as he saw him. Talk about a small world."

Bernie smiled. "No, son, it's a small galaxy."

Then they watched in silence as the shuttle pod carrying Shakespeare and Bernie's father lifted off. It began to grow gradually smaller and smaller until it was lost against the azure, cloudless sky.

Survivors

May 5, 1955
Nevada Test Site - Operation Teapot - Test Apple-2

THOUGH HE WAS WEARING PROTECTIVE GOGGLES—he had been assured the dark lenses would protect his eyes—Lieutenant JG Edward Dugan still averted his eyes when a flash as bright as the sun lit up the early morning sky over the test site. When he crouched below the bunker wall, he pressed his trembling hand against the cool steel that was two feet thick and covered by earth. The steel was becoming warmer with each passing second.

The hushed voices of the senior officers and scientists around him helped to keep his fear buried.

They didn't sound afraid as he was, only more in awe of the force of the blast created by the exploded atom bomb.

A faint taste of acidic bile from the back of Edward's throat and his heart pounding against his ribs reminded him he was still alive.

"Quite a show, eh, Dugan?"

Edward glanced to his right to see General Marks peering through the slit opening along one bunker wall, his binoculars trained on the blast site. The bunker windows were made of special glass. In order to stop the radiation. The glass was made with a mixture consisting of twenty six percent lead. The viewing window was inches thick sufficient to protect anyone looking out through the slit from flying debris.

The general dropped to his haunches as the roar of the blast wave swept over the bunker like a vengeful, super-heated spirit. High-speed winds peppered the bunker with rocks and dirt.

Though he'd never experienced actual combat, Edward imagined the sound was like being attacked by enemy machine guns.

A loud *thud* announced the arrival of debris from Survival Town, the artificial town specifically constructed for the test.

General Marks offered him a lopsided grin. The oval lenses of the dark goggles glinted in the pale golden glow of the emergency lights in the ceiling of the bunker. Over six feet in height, General Marks had always seemed a giant to Edward, who stood five feet ten in his GI-issue boots.

Marks had won the Congressional Medal of Honor in Korea for leading his troops in a successful battle at Hill 402, where they routed three companies of Chinese regulars, and he had been a decorated company captain in Europe during World War II. The guy was a real-life war hero. Now as a general, he was in charge of Operation Teapot to further test atomic weapons in case they were needed against America's latest enemy: the dreaded Reds.

Edward had been too young for Korea, never mind the Second World War. His job was as General Marks' aide. The thought of using atomic weapons terrified him.

At last the howling winds waned and the rapid, pelting sounds abated.

Marks shoved his goggles up his dirt-streaked forehead, revealing his icy blue eyes; the corners wrinkled as he smiled. "Dugan," he began, "I want you to take a couple of men and go check Survival Town for me.

I want a quick on-site assessment of the damage before these egg heads..."

With a slight nod of his head, he indicated the four scientists in civilian garb, huddled together in one corner of the bunker. "...are escorted into the area."

The scientists stood next to a pine table brimming with Geiger counters and other measuring devices Edward didn't recognize (and had been told the knowledge of which was well above his pay grade).

"Yes, sir." Edward was glad to be leaving the bunker. Being confined in enclosed spaces had made him uncomfortable ever since the time his older brother locked him in a closet when he was five.

Edward quickly recruited two privates, one to drive the jeep. They were soon roaring across the parched prairie toward the shattered, twisted remains of the artificial town built to assess damage from an atomic blast. Every detail had been considered.

Department stores dummies stood in for actual humans, some as children playing outside; houses were complete with furniture; even stuffed animals represented family pets. The hastily constructed houses had been set up in the town as if a sudden attack by the reds had occurred.

Edward had heard of civilians building their own survival bunkers in their backyards and basements, hoping they'd survive the war everyone expected would occur.

As the jeep bounced over the uneven landscape, Edward saw the desert had been scoured clean of cacti and scrub brush. Every living thing had been wiped away by blowing dirt and sand as if by the hand of a vengeful God. In some places there were charred plants and blackened sand, some spots shiny where the sudden burst of intense heat had turned the sand to glass. He shuddered at the thought of living people being stuck out here when a bomb such as this exploded.

Finally the jeep approached the shadows of streets of the destroyed town to find buildings collapsed in heaps of blackened wood, mannequins burned and scarred, with arms and legs gone or heads missing. They drove slowly past a children's tricycle, the frame bent and twisted; telephone poles askew at odd angles; and a speed limit sign with one corner folded back, the sign at a forty-five-degree angle, but still partially buried in the ground.

Edward swallowed hard as they passed ever-increasing damage, each more horrific than the next, until his breath caught in his throat.

Survivors

He stared at something that made his heart freeze. "Stop!" he shouted.

The driver stepped hard on the brake and the jeep screeched to a shuddering stop, the brakes squealing loudly.

There in the center of the town square at the junction where three streets intersected stood what appeared to be three flesh-and-blood children: one blonde girl wearing a pink party dress and two boys in dungarees and striped tee shirts, none of whom appeared to be older than ten.

They were unharmed. Their clothing bore no sign of charring, their hair was perfectly combed, not a strand out of place. They appeared to be clean, unharmed. Somehow they had survived a blast of an atomic bomb.

Edward gaped at the children, standing in a circle holding hands with their eyes closed. His mind didn't believe what his brown eyes were seeing.

Impossible.

***

May 10, 1985
Boston, Massachusetts - Julien Bar, Hotel
Meridien

Ellen McKee sipped her second peach sidecar
of the evening. Looking around the smoky bar, she
saw that Peter and Rupert were scoping out the local
talent as they did every Friday when the staff of the
advertising firm of Heston, Queen, and Bradbury
reconvened their meetings at Julien's after working
hours.

Ellen sat alone at the table she'd been sharing
with her colleagues for the past forty minutes,
enjoying their initial warm-up drink of the evening
together. Now was the time to prowl.

She smiled to herself as the burn of the cognac
slid across her tongue, followed by the tang of the
orange liqueur and lastly the sweet peach juice. She
loved these weekly get-togethers. She also loved the
idea of trolling for a rumpy-pumpy each week. But a
good man was hard to find.

And a new man is even harder to find, she thought,
scanning the predominantly male clientele and seeing
the many equally recognizable and forgettable faces
in the crowded bar.

Survivors

Her ex-husband, Albert, would have hated the Julien Bar, with its comfortable, tanned couches and overstuffed leather chairs scattered across the hardwood floors. The stone fireplace against one wall added warmth to the dimly lit space. A wall of mirrors, filled with shelves of liquors from all over the world, reflected the eager faces of men and women determined not go home alone, leaning on the smooth, black surface of the onyx bar in front of the mirrors many smoking cigarettes, something she'd never enjoyed.

The Julien was located in the basement of the hotel, so there were no windows.

No, Albert would have never come into such a place as this. He liked roadside bars with scarred pine tables and rickety chairs with ripped seat cushions. A spittoon and an old, mangy dog lying next to the wood-burning stove would complete Albert's dream bar.

The barrage of voices generated by the crowd of business-suited professionals spread out across the bar—some of the bar's occupants were seated on the chairs and couches, others standing in tight groups arguing, no doubt, about some sports or political big deal of the day—would have driven Albert crazy.

Maybe it was the buzz created by the alcohol, but she felt pretty good tonight. *I deserve a good time*, she thought.

She smiled into her glass. As she tipped it back to take another sip, the smell of the alcohol and juice invaded her nostrils. A light tap on her left shoulder made the lust rise from within her.

Lowering the glass, she shifted in her seat to look to her left and was startled to discover a red-haired woman dressed in a navy pantsuit and a white cotton blouse. Behind her stood a very large man with the shoulders of a Patriots linebacker, wearing a similar dark suit, only with a red tie down the front of his ivory-colored shirt. The woman's flat brown eyes gazed at her, making Ellen vaguely uncomfortable, all thoughts of sexual conquest having fled.

"Yes?" Ellen asked, her speech slightly slurred.

"Are you Ellen Thomas?"

Ellen grunted dismissively. "I used to be. I'm Ellen McKee now." Her eyes narrowed as she set her glass on the table. "What do you want?"

The woman's thin lips formed a tight smile that didn't reach her eyes. "Who says I want something?"

Ellen chuckled, her voice edged with bitterness. "In my experience, lady, *everyone* has an angle."

The woman shrugged her narrow shoulders; her suit jacket opened enough so Ellen could see a holster hidden under her jacket attached to her belt. Ellen's mouth dried and her heart skipped a beat. *Government.*

The woman reached into her jacket pocket and pulled out a black leather wallet. She flipped it open, revealing a badge and an identification card. "I'm Agent Ayres." She paused to nod at the man-mountain standing behind her, listening quietly, his features impassive, his hands folded in front of him. "This is Agent Corday. We're with the National Security Agency." The wallet disappeared in her jacket. "We'd like you to come with us."

Ellen's green eyes flitted between the two government agents. *Why are they bothering me again, after all this time?* She sighed and her shoulders slumped. "Listen, Agent Ayres, I've been questioned many times and I have nothing more I can add. I don't remember how I got there—"

"Hold on please, ma'am. I don't know what you're talking about. That information is above our pay grade. Our job is to accompany you to the airport, where a plane is waiting."

Ellen stared into Agent Ayres' eyes, trying to determine if she should believe her. Maybe, after all this time, they were going to assassinate her once she left the bar...and the others. But it didn't seem right. Why would they bother to talk to her? Why not just take her out in an unexplained *accident?*

Of course, what worried Ellen more than dying was the plane's destination. She could refuse to go with them, only Ayres didn't actually mean they were sent to *accompany* her. Ellen knew the agents would hog-tie her if necessary and drag her to the airport.

She had no choice.

***

May 11, 1985
Thirty thousand feet over the Nevada desert

Ellen yawned as she awoke in the enveloping comfort of the soft leather seat. She was the only passenger in a cabin that could hold twenty people. The smell of leather and men's aftershave was strong. The pilots were in the cockpit behind the door at the front of the passenger compartment.

Survivors

Looking down at the cup holder in the armrest of her seat, she saw her glass of vodka was gone. *Bastards took my drink.*

She smacked her lips. Her mouth tasted dry and sticky, probably due to the fifth of vodka she'd consumed last night. The corporate jet, with blackout windows, no markings on its white fuselage—other than a tail number in black and a red stripe down both sides of the plane—was well stocked with supplies for a government jet.

During the ride to the airport in a limousine—which felt more like they were at the Indy 500, they were driving so fast—Ayers kept insisting they knew nothing about the plane's final destination. (Ellen thought her partner Corday might be a robot due to his continued silence.)

Ellen thought Ayers was lying. Two armed government agents playing delivery jerks for one slightly overweight, drunken, nearly-forty-year-old woman. Their mission, to get her in a flying taxi to nowhere? It didn't make sense.

Shrugging off the question, knowing she wasn't going to get any answers by staying in Boston, Ellen boarded the plane and managed to take full advantage of the time it would take to get to wherever the plane was headed by appropriating some of the booze supply for her own personal use.

Ellen suspected the plane was headed for Groom Lake, where she'd been taken after "the event," as she called it. Somehow she'd never been able to call it the atomic bomb test, or Project Teapot, as she later learned the weapons test was called.

A violent bump jerked her forward in her seat, forcing her to hold one hand out and press it into the seat in front of her to keep from being thrown to the floor. Her stomach heaved and she burped. Her nose wrinkled as the blend of perspiration and stale booze wafted over her.

I must smell like a booze factory after an earthquake.

Glancing above her head, she saw the seatbelt light had come on, glowing red. The cabin lights suddenly went out, throwing the cabin into blackness. Her fingers cramping due to dehydration, she grabbed both ends of the seat belt and after struggling to bring them together, she finally managed to click it into place just before the aircraft suddenly tipped sharply to the left. The steady thrumming of the engines died away. Ellen's heart leapt to her throat and she swallowed a scream.

Oh, God, no. I'm going to die…

She became weightless as the plane began to drop rapidly, losing altitude at an ever-increasing rate. The seat belt dug into her flesh, making her grimace in pain. Closing her eyes, Ellen said a silent prayer, her hands gripping the seat arms. As the aircraft's speed steadily increased, her seat belt struggled to keep her from flying upward into the ceiling.

Puffing her cheeks, she attempted to suck in air—but the seatbelt tightened around her waist making breathing seem impossible. Her thoughts became muddled and foggy as her mind drifted to her ex-husband and the love they once shared. She hoped she'd be unconscious before the plane crashed. Her mother had died such an agonizingly slow death from bone cancer; Ellen wanted a quick exit. This might be her time. "I'm so sorry, Albert...really..." she whispered. "I love you, Mom."

As quickly as it started, the feeling of weightless decreased as the plane leveled off. But the engine noise hadn't returned. She opened her eyes and saw the overhead lights had come on again. What was happening?

"This is your pilot. Prepare for landing. It might be a little bumpy and we'll have to brake hard after touchdown, but don't be concerned."

Russ Crossley

Ellen thought she heard tautness in the pilot's tone that might be fear, but she decided she was imagining things. It is better not to think that the pilot of the plane you're a passenger on is as scared as you are. "You've had a stressful day," she murmured under her breath to reassure herself, then swallowed hard.

A sharp bump jarred her, then threw her upward against the seat belt, which again cut into her already painful belly flesh. She winced and held her breath. This was followed by a steadily decreasing series of bumps, the aircraft bouncing wildly beneath her. She was tossed hard left, then hard right in her seat as the aircraft swayed side to side.

She was thrown forward when the breaks were applied, staying in her seat only because of her seat belt. In order to keep from hitting the seat in front of her, she pressed her hands into the seat back.

The screech of tires on pavement was followed by the bang of the galley doors springing open behind her and the crash of bottles, glasses, and garbage cans flinging onto the cabin floor.

Finally the plane rolled to a stop and Ellen began to breath again, sucking in deep breaths, trying to steady her heart rate back to some semblance of normal. Not that any part of this was normal.

The pilot's voice came over the cabin speaker again. "I'll be opening the doors in two minutes. Your escort has just arrived."

What, no thank you for flying Crap-Your-Pants airlines? thought Ellen.

She wondered if she should have agreed to come on this trip at all. Maybe she should have called the cops when the agents showed up. But no doubt the NSA had thought of this and had an agreement with the local cops. *They own me.*

The plane's exit door swung upward as Ellen made her way forward between the rows of seats, her low heels digging into the plush maroon carpet lining the cabin deck.

Bright sunlight streamed through the door, making her eyes water and blinding her momentarily until she blinked and brought one hand up to shade her eyes.

She stepped to the top of the ladder that extended to the cracked tarmac. A wave of heat washed over her causing beads of perspiration to immediately pop from on her upper lip and forehead. She wished now she'd brought her sunglasses. Her vision quickly cleared. At the bottom of the stairs were two uniformed air force officers, gazing up at her. Parked behind them was an enclosed jeep with its motor still running.

The taller of the two men had steel gray hair visible around the edges of his peaked cap. She decided that he was the senior of the two officers. Brass and service ribbons covered his left jacket pocket, indicating he'd been in the armed forces for a very long time. Reflective aviator sunglasses hid his eyes. The shorter of the two men wore the same sunglasses, but his chest contained very few service ribbons and no brass.

She carefully walked down the stairs, her legs still trembling from the near-death experience and the booze.

Finally she stood on the tarmac, barely able to stop herself from kneeling and kissing the ground.

"Ellen?" asked the older officer with all the ribbons and colorful accoutrements decorating his chest, his thin lips forming a wide smile.

Peering at his shoulders, she saw two silver stars on each side. The guy was a general. Her eyes flitted to the younger of the two officers to see a single bar on each of his bony shoulders. She knew shit about military ranks but the young one had to be the junior officer. Probably the big man's aide or something.

"Uh, yeah. I'm Ellen McKee." Her eyes narrowed. *How does this man know my name?* "Who are you?"

Survivors

The general removed his sunglasses, revealing warm brown eyes, the flesh beside them crinkled due to his wide grin. "It's me." He must have seen the lack of comprehension in her eyes because he chuckled and stepped forward to wrap her in his arms, hugging her to him. "Ed Dugan."

Ellen was stunned. *Ed?* She hadn't seen or heard from him in almost thirty years.

After *the event* in '55 when she was taken to Groom Air Force Base, she was accompanied— there's that word again—by Lieutenant Edward Dugan, a pimply-faced kid who claimed to be an officer. She'd only been nine years old at the time, but even then, Ed hadn't looked too much older than her.

Back then he'd been a jumpy, nervous, junior officer around her and the others. The others being Milt Swag and Ben Kwong who, so she was told later, had been with her at *the event*. The three had been at the epicenter of a blast by an atomic bomb that flattened Survivor Town and demonstrated the shocking destruction wrought by a weapon of mass destruction too terrible to be used.

During the cold war that followed, the United States and the U.S.S.R. were fearful of Mutual Assured Destruction, also known as MAD, because both sides recognized nuclear war was unwinnable.

After atomic bomb test Apple-2 in May of 1955, a few people would have disagreed since three seemingly normal children survived a holocaust of a destruction that should have vaporized them and no one knew why or how they'd survived or even why they were there. Not even she, Milt, or Ben had the answers to these questions. But Ellen badly wanted to know. That day had consumed most of her waking hours ever since and was the principal reason she drank. Unfortunately, their memories of what had happened to them had somehow been erased.

The three children had been reported missing by their parents two days before the bomb test, but all Ellen remembered of the time before she arrived at Groom Lake was playing with her dog in the front yard of her parents house. Milt and Ben had pretty much the same story.

The U.S. government had kept the incident secret since that day in 1955 and had sworn the children and their parents to secrecy by threatening them with life imprisonment for treason if they ever revealed their part in test Apple-2.

Now here was that same nervous lieutenant, now a general, welcoming her as if she were some long-lost friend. The mint of his mouthwash and the tang of his musky aftershave filled her nose.

Finally he released her, with his hands still grasping her shoulders.

"How have you been?' he asked, his expression eager as a schoolboy.

"Uhhh...confused?"

General Dugan laughed. He dropped his hands to his sides. "Of course you are...I'm sorry..." He turned toward the pasty-faced, thin-as-a-toothpick, young officer who stood impassively watching them. "This is my aide, Lieutenant Mitchell, but ignore him. He's me thirty years ago."

The general laughed loudly at his joke, while Mitchell's brow wrinkled and his hazel eyes narrowed slightly. He then emitted a brief chuckle.

"Very good, sir," he said in a low monotone.

Dugan scoffed at his aide. "Of course it's good. I said it, Mitchell." He started to walk toward the waiting jeep. "Let's get out of here. We don't have much time.

"Sorry about the rough landing, Ellen; that seems to happen around her quite a bit. Folks get a little upset, but don't worry; it's perfectly normal."

Boy, has he changed, thought Ellen following after him. *He's been promoted to arrogant jerk.*

When she arrived at the jeep, Mitchell was holding the rear passenger door open for her.

She climbed in and slid across the cloth seat. The interior of the jeep was much cooler than the oppressive desert heat outside. General Dugan climbed into the front passenger seat and his aide took the driver's seat.

Her eyes traveled to the mist-covered mountains in the distance across a barren, unforgiving landscape dotted with cacti and scrub brush. Waves of heat shimmered in the distance creating the illusion of water.

Memories of suddenly becoming aware of these surroundings flooded back, threatening to overwhelm her with the force of the memories of the fear, dread, and shock she'd felt on the day she found herself standing amongst the ruins of Survivor Town.

Looking ahead she could still see the ghost-like outline of the road that had led to the faux town thirty years ago.

"General, is this Survivor Town?" she asked.

General Dugan, who had his back to her as the jeep jerked into movement, the engine roaring in the confined space, turned to look at her, his eyes hard now. "Yes, at least where it used to be. We're headed for the spot where you, Milt, and Ben were found."

"Why?"

It was a simple question, one that had haunted her in many ways since that day, the day that changed the course of her life. Gazing into this now-old man's eyes, she knew his life had also been transformed by the experience. He had obviously had success in the military hierarchy, but something more was behind those eyes. Something he wasn't about to share with her or probably anyone. Much like her, Dugan was damaged goods.

When the jeep came to a stop, there were two jeeps already parked at a junction of three roads forming the spot known as ground zero. There was a group of men standing talking at the center of the junction. Some were in uniform, some in civilian garb.

Ellen swung open the door and climbed out, again struck by how hot it was. Mitchell was thoughtful enough to hand her a pair of sunglasses like those he and the general were wearing.

Her heart suddenly almost leapt from her chest when she spotted two familar faces amongst the knot of men. The faces were older, fuller to be sure, but unmistakable. Ben and Milt were here, too.

Racing across the road, she threw her arms around Ben and hugged him. With tears staining her cheeks, she released him, then did the same to Milt.

They, too, were driven to tears by the sudden reunion. They had shared an experience like none other in history.

Ellen gathered herself and released Milt. They gazed at each other happily between a blur of tears, unable to speak.

"Ten minutes, sir," said Mitchell from where he stood to their right near the jeep that had brought Ellen to this spot.

Ellen stopped crying and turned to glare at Dugan. "What's really going on, General?"

Dugan avoided her stare. "Well, you see, we've never been certain how you three survived the blast and we thought if we brought you here again when we tested a new weapon system, we might learn your secret."

Ellen looked to the other two survivors. Both Ben's and Milt's eyes registered their surprise and confusion. She looked back at Dugan. "Do you mean you *hope* we'll survive?"

Dugan nodded. "Listen, I'm sorry about this, but surely you don't think we can just let it go and not try to determine why you all survived the blast in '55. We have to know how you did it."

"So you can build a newer, better defensive system, or maybe a weapon to better kill commies? Correct?" Ellen asked, her eyes narrowing. She had never trusted these bastards.

Dugan nodded.

Mitchell walked up to him carrying an attaché case. He laid it on the hood of one of the jeeps and opened it. Inside were three smooth gray stones, scarred with markings etched into the surface of the stones.

"We still have these."

She watched his Adam's apple bob as he swallowed. "We found you three holding them in your hands after we discovered you in this exact spot. We've run every test on them we know and they came back exactly as what they appear: inert rock. Unremarkable in every way."

Ellen stared at the stones resting in cloth pockets in the case and something came over her. Fog crept in from the sides of her eyes, blurring first her vision, then clouding her mind. The oppressive heat, the desert, the men, the rush of the steady breeze blowing grains of fine sand across her cheeks, her friends—everything and everyone disappeared in the fog.

May 8, 2015

Apartment 16D - Bayview Apartments - Boston, Massachusetts

The television's volume was set low while Ellen worked on her latest knitting project. Sandra Lebowski and her husband Adam in apartment 8A were having their first child soon and she wanted to finish the knitted sleeper before the baby arrived. Ellen liked Sandy and Adam. They were a nice couple.

Her eyes drifted up to the television screen while her fingers worked the knitting needles. Castle had just described one of his preposterous theories of the crime. She chuckled to herself. The guy was *so* handsome, and *so* dumb.

The intercom buzzer sounded, interrupting her thoughts. Sighing, she stood and ambled to the intercom, set in the wall next to the hallway door. Pressing the red button, she activated the speaker. "Hello?" She released the button so whoever was at the other end could speak.

"It's Agent Wilson of the NSA, ma'am. We're here to pick you up for your flight."

Ellen rolled her eyes, then pressed the button again. "Okay. I'll be down in ten minutes." Releasing the button, she ambled to the bedroom to collect her small overnight bag. She wasn't about to be unprepared this time.

Of course, it helped this time that the general had called her in advance, telling her they were testing a particle beam weapon. From his description, the weapon would make for one hell of a big punch. He said it might actually penetrate the shield. Good for the military, bad for them.

Time was growing short.

The alien attack force had entered the solar system. Ellen, Milt, and Ben had agreed to make the ultimate sacrifice if it would save the human race from annihilation.

But like much of the human race, they were survivors.

She hadn't had a drink of alcohol since that day in 1985—she didn't want her mind clouded by anything she could control ever again—after the space defense system weapons test, or as the press called it, Star Wars, named after the energy weapons depicted in the popular science fiction movie series.

Every few years the military took her and the others to the weapons testing ground to test their latest weapon of mass destruction, hoping they'd learn the truth behind the stones. And they hoped to discover why she, Ben, and Milt were able to survive the destruction of the newest model of death ray, or whatever, created by the next generation of mad scientists. The government was becoming increasingly desperate due to the looming threat to the planet.

She turned off the television and collected her pre-packed suitcase, rolling it across her carpeted floor on its wheels to the front closet, where she retrieved her thin nylon windbreaker and slipped on her open-toed leather sandals.

Taking one last look around her one bedroom apartment, she doubted she'd see her home again. If this test failed, she was convinced the government would dissect her and the others. They needed the secret of their survival, even if it meant cutting them open to get it.

She smirked as she opened the door and walked into the hall. The problem was, she wanted answers too. Even if she had to die to get them.

Survivors

She could refuse to go, but she knew she had no choice; and General Mitchell hated to be kept waiting.

The door closed behind her with a dull *thump*.

About the Author

International selling author, Russ Crossley writes science fiction and fantasy, and mystery/suspense as well as their various subgenres.

His latest science fiction satire set in the far future, Revenge of the Lushites, is a sequel to Attack of the Lushites released in 2011. The latest title in the series was released in the fall of 2013. Both titles are available in e-book and trade paperback.

He has sold several short stories that have appeared in anthologies from various publishers including; WMG Publishing, Pocket Books, 53rd Street Publishing, and St. Martins Press.

He is a member of SF Canada and is past president of the Greater Vancouver Chapter of Romance Writers of America. He is also an alumni of the Oregon Coast Professional Fiction Writers Master Class taught by award winning author/editors, Kristine Katherine Rusch and Dean Wesley Smith.

Feel free to contact him on Facebook, Twitter, or his website http//:www.russcrossley.com. He loves to hear from readers.

Other titles from 53rd Street Publishing you
may enjoy
http://www.53rdstreetpublising.com

Other books by the Author

Razor and Edge Mysteries
The Kidnapping of Billy Buttons
String of Pearls
Death by Clown
Beggin' For Murder
Ragged Ice
The Grand Central Mystery
A Strange Case of Undead Murder

Jazz Stiletto Mysteries
A Day Without Sunshine
Skullduggery
Instrument of justice (first published in Over My
Dead Body online mystery magazine)

The Amanda Dark paranormal mysteries
Hook Island
Grind Manor
Moonrise Diner
A Father's Daughter

The Trudy Wilson Mystery Novel Series
Bad Loyalty
Shear Murder
Buzzcut - coming soon

Other Novels

Attack of the Lushites
Revenge of the Lushites
My Zombie Prince
Antique Virgin
The Fire In Their Hearts
with R.S. Meger (from Champagne Books)
Zomopolis
The Last Serial Killer

Short Stories
Countdown
Shoeless Moe
Round Up At The Burger Bar:
The Story of Trixie Pug, Parts 1, 2, 3, 4, 5, 6, 7, 8, 9
Five Minutes
Blossom Queen, Barbarian
The Secret
The Family Line
End of the Flies
Death by Magic
The Penguin Sleeps With The Fishes
Only The Worthy
Hero For A Day
End of Empire
Strange Bedfellows
Big Business
A Perfect Crime
The Wise Guy and The Pirates
In Search of the Perfect Cup
T.I.N. Men

The Legend of G and the Dragonettes
The Incredible Mr. Fix-It
Lock Stock and Barrel
Divided Loyalties
Cave of Wonders
A Family Empire
Until We Meet Again
Dragon Rising
Solitary Man
The Keel Mountain Conspiracy
Angel on My Shoulder
Heroes of Old
The Great Bicycle Race
Tikka's Big Day
"My Partner the Zombie" —
Hungry For Your Love Anthology
(St. Martin's Press)
Big Hairy Deal
One Red Shoe
A Bad Day in Lunden Texas
Bloody Betty, Queen of the Pirates
Mirror Image
Dangerous Waters
Cape Disappointment
Boomerang
The Watcher of Wayburn Street
The Apprentice
Drip!
A Beautiful Friendship and The Parrot of Doom
Robine's Diary
The Christmas Club
Loose Ends

Splatter Pattern
It Takes Two
Lexicon
Replacement Parts
Sidekicks
Lost Stories
Time and Space
Survivors
Neighborhood Watch
Unnatural Immortal
Rum Runner's Lounge
It's A Small Galaxy
A Shattered Man
Betrayed
Replacement Parts
Clubhouse Heroes
Sounds That Angels Make
Muggins Rules – originally published in Fiction River
Volume 12, Risk Takers

Anthologies
Tales of Urban Fantasy
Five Tales of Bizarre Detectives
Tales of Mystery and Suspense
Tales of Weird Fantasy
Spies, Detectives, & Heroes
Tales of Twisted Crime
Tales of The Unexpected
Tales From Space
10 by Russ Crossley
Round Up At The Burger Bar: The Story of Trixie
Pug,

Parts 1- 5 The Beginning
Worlds of Science Fiction and Fantasy
More Tales of Mystery and Suspense
Ladies of the Jolly Roger
Justice Served
Love Stories
Ladies of the Jolly Roger with Rita Schulz
The Adventures of Razor and Edge:
Five Tales From The Quirky Detective Team
An Unexpected Journey
On Edge
Thrilling Adventures
Total War

Non-Fiction
The Writers Tools - The Synopsis

Tales of alternate worlds where steam and alchemy mix during a race between empires, journey to a far off world on the other side of the galaxy where an ancient desperate struggle between good and evil is being fought. A story concerning a boy who has his own guardian angel. A story where you will discover a secret world hidden beneath our own where being odd is a virtue, and journey across the galaxy where an artificial intelligence decides the future of the human race.

Included in this volume is a new story about paranormal investigator, Amanda Dark, and her continuing investigations into the dark corners of death where others fear to tread in the chilling tale, Moonrise Diner.

Check out this volume of extraordinary tales of mystery and the paranormal, these Unexpected Journey's

A mysterious discovery off the coast of South Africa puts Dane Maddock and his intrepid crew on the trail of a legendary hero, and in the crosshairs of a deadly international conspiracy bent on keeping that discovery hidden forever.

PRAISE FOR DAVID WOOD AND THE DANE MADDOCK ADVENTURES!

A great read that provides lots of action, and thoughtful insight as well, into strange realms that are sometimes best left unexplored." Paul Kemprecos, author of Cool Blue Tomb

"Dane and Bones.... Together they're unstoppable. Rip-roaring action from start to finish. Wit and humor throughout. Just one question - how soon until the next one? Because I can't wait." Graham Brown, author of Shadows of the Midnight Sun

"David Wood has done it again. Quest takes you on an expedition that leads down a trail of adventure and thrills!" David L. Golemon, Author of the Event Group series

"Ancient cave paintings? Cities of gold? Secret scrolls? Sign me up! A twisty tale of adventure and intrigue that never lets up and never lets go!" Robert Masello, author of The Medusa Amulet

It was hard enough being a teenager but when you have special abilities…

After begging and pleading—I texted Mark, Spike, and Ach every ten minutes for the rest of the day until they agreed I should come—I convinced the guys to let me join the club at the park. Not that they could stop me, since this is a public event and I'm still part of the public.

What disappointed me the most was Izzy's attitude. She didn't seem to care if I came along or not. It was actually Mark who seemed to be the only one concerned about my safety.

Anyway, when we arrived at the park the place was jammed with people, their kids and dogs running wild all over the tramped down grass which probably would be dead until next spring. Not that this was my problem, but I enjoy green grass and the smell when it's fresh cut. All right I'm weird, what can I say?